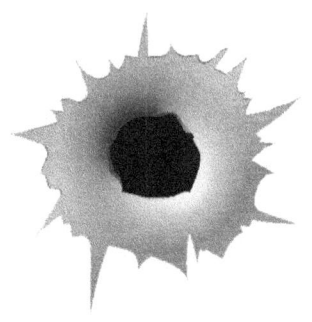

TONY CAPRA

ORGANIZED CRIME BOSS

ISBN 978-1-62806-417-9 (print | paperback)

Library of Congress Control Number 2024916258

Published by Salt Water Media
29 Broad Street, Suite 104
Berlin, MD 21811
www.saltwatermedia.com

Editor: Patsy Myles

Disclaimer: The contents written in this book are purely fictional, and any resemblance to anyone alive or dead is a coincidence only.

TONY CAPRA

ORGANIZED CRIME BOSS

Joe Myles

AUTHOR'S NOTE

From an early age, Tony was determined to become a person of importance when he became a man. He didn't have a clue how this would be accomplished, or even know what a person of importance was. All little Tony knew was that he wanted more of everything he didn't have now. Time will tell if he ever achieves his goal.

CONTENTS

The Tony Capra Story 11

The Early Days 14

Life on My Block 18

Mom's Family 24

Self-Employment 31

Tough Times 34

Jersey Family Visits 37

The Maryland Move 41

Girlfriend Experience 44

High School - Crime 101 48

Learning the Business 53

Atlantic City Move 56

Johnny Rinzo 58

Providing An Example 61

Tiers of Power 63

Casinos in Atlantic City 67

Kelly's Bar 70

My Girls 74

Casino Owner 76

Expanding Territory 79

White Powder 83

Opposite Direction 85

Mafia Fears 91

Turn of Events 92

Safe House 95

Senator Capra 97

A Move on the Mob 99

A Snitch 103

New York Gang War 106

Hit Again 109

The Next Plan 111

THE TONY CAPRA STORY

"**O**ur gift of bread so that this house may never know hunger, and this gift of salt so that your lives may always have flavor, and this bottle of wine to ensure that joy and prosperity may reign forever." That is how every first visit to our Italian family or friends began when we entered a new home they had just moved into, regardless of whether the home was a new or an old house; and whether they were buying or renting. This was to be their new home, for a few months, a few years, or their entire lifetime. This home was destined to be their central gathering place to start and end each day; the location where most meals would be consumed, and the meeting place where small and large decisions on how to go forward in their lives would be discussed and determined. The protection of the family's lives and belongings were important reasons for the shelter, but the home is where the family nurturing and growth day by day, from birth until death, forms the personality and stature of each individual.

On this particular cool and bright sunny day in October of 1954, my family, the Capra's, consisting of my parents, four sisters and myself were exploring our new house we had just moved into the prior week. This row house in Philadelphia was Papa's very first house purchase, and the cost at about Ten Thousand Dollars seemed to us a huge fortune. Before moving we had been living in a house Papa's father owned on Chester Avenue, which was a duplex that had an apartment downstairs and one apartment upstairs. My Uncle Gus and Aunt Marie and cousin Gianni lived downstairs and we lived upstairs, which worked out fine for us all to have family that close. Gianni and I were the same age which gave us both an automatic playmate. My sisters had to contend with each other for their playmates since there just weren't any neighbor children close by. Now that we were in our new house our social lives would be much different. We hadn't had any playmates on Chester Avenue and we now had an entire street full of kids of all ages. Our new street was named Reinhard Street, and I was told it was the longest city block in Philadelphia. I had no doubt this was true. It certainly was the center of my universe in those early days. The statistic that really meant more to me than the length of the street was that there were many, many kids of all ages living in those row houses on that long street who would provide playmates for me and my sisters. It was a very long narrow one-lane, one-way street that had curb parking on the right side. There were row houses on each side with a variety of styles of porch railings separating each of the houses. Everyone on the street had the same basic house: a three-story narrow building with a cellar, a dirt or concrete backyard only large enough only to have a clothes line for hanging laundry to dry. Every row house shared the wall on each side with the next door neighbor, so the entire street was actually one building. Although the footprint of each house was the same, many of the neighbors had made alterations to their houses over the years. For instance the choice of dirt or concrete backyard. When the houses were built they came with dirt and some owners had concrete poured later. Other improvements like a storage shed or an addition on the back of the house were built by a few people that had money. Several of the tenants had converted their front porches into enclosed rooms with windows to keep out of the elements year round. Or they converted the porches into additional living area. The only thing Papa did to alter our house was to convert the square openings from the living room to the dining room, and the opening from the dining room to the kitchen from the routine squared off corners by adding arches for each of them. Since he was a plasterer by trade, he applied his expertise and made forms for each space and then cut and applied the screening to hold the brown coat which was the base that held the bright white plaster. The project could not be completed in one day due to the necessary drying period for the brown coat, but when it was time to apply the finish coat Papa mixed the plaster in a pan as large as a small bathtub. He looked like an artist painting the Sistine Chapel. Working overhead with his arm muscles bulging, he held a flat metal tray fitted with a wooden handle piled high with plaster in one hand, and the trowel he held in his right hand was used to apply the plaster over the brown coat. I watched him as every pass of his plaster-filled trowel skimmed onto the arch transforming the rough square opening into a classic work of art. It was later that I realized he made the arches for my Mom. But also by doing that, he made his mark on his new home.

13

THE EARLY DAYS

One fall night we were sitting around our dining table in our new house having our evening meal when we heard the door open and close. Nobody ever locked their front doors. I never even knew why they even bothered to put locks on the them.

I don't know what everyone else thought, but I just assumed it was one of our friends, or the next door neighbor. It wasn't. Instead my Aunt Rita and my Mom's brother Uncle Nunzio from Cherry Hill, New Jersey appeared in the doorway of the kitchen. Dinner came to a halt as we got up from the table and greeted them. Immediately after everyone swapped hugs and kisses my mom asked them "Jeet?" (Did you eat?) After they automatically declined my Uncle reached into his bag, pulled out a long loaf of Italian bread and started reciting the Bread, Salt and Wine blessing for our new Home. This was of course directed towards my parents since we were taught that when grownups were present our place was off to the side and we were expected to be quiet, and to speak only when spoken to. After a fair amount of time was spent with the adults catching up with their lives since they last met, attention was turned towards the kids, especially the girls. Out of another bag they brought with them, Aunt Rita started pulling out gifts for us. The girls each received a dress-up doll, and of course the dolls were all different from each other. After they gave their polite thank you's and went off to play with them, it was my turn. Aunt Rita reached in the bag and came out with a Western six-shooter pistol for me that had it's own holster and a little box of red roll caps to shoot. This was a perfect gift for any boy because the most popular television shows we watched were westerns such as Hopalong Cassidy, the cowboy that wore a black and white handkerchief around his neck, and rode a white horse. Another program I looked forward to was the Lone Ranger television program that featured a former Texas Ranger. He wore a black eye mask and had an Indian friend named Tonto. His horse was named Silver. We also watched the Cisco Kid, who had a partner named Pancho. We looked forward to the end of each episode when they would turn to each other and Cisco would say, "Aw Pancho" and Pancho would say, "Aw Cisco" and then laugh. Of course there was Roy Rogers, the King of the Cowboys. His real wife, Dale, co-starred with him. I really enjoyed this part of the visit, it seemed the longer the time since the last visit, the larger the gifts we would receive. After receiving our gifts, Mom put us kids back at the dinner table to finish our meals while the grownups opened the ceremonial wine that was brought for the toast and continued their conversations. I suppose after the visit that house became a home.

Then there were the visits from Papa's father. Bubba was the name we called that grandfather. He had a driver's license and a car so he was able to visit often to check in on us, and we knew he usually would also be bearing presents on his visits. He would sometimes bring us an educational children's book, or just bring us some treats of candy. The size of the present didn't matter to us. Bubba and my Grandmother "Mumma" lived about fifteen minutes from us in Upper Darby, a suburb of Philadelphia. We considered my grandparents rich judging from the house they lived in and the shiny big black DeSoto Bubba drove. My grandfather Benito Capra was born in Taormino, Sicily and came to America for a better life. He was hired as an apprentice in the plastering trade, and worked his way to the top and became the International President of the Plasterers Union. In this capacity he had to make frequent trips from Philadelphia to Washington, D.C. where he kept a room at the Madison Hotel on Fourteenth Street near the White House. Mumma didn't travel with him on the business trips. In fact she didn't make the short jaunts to visit us when Bubba made his visits. She kept very busy at home with her daily duties of cleaning house, washing clothes and most importantly preparing meals. We did visit with her at their house at least once each week. Papa would drive her to church every Sunday and the rest of us would stay at their house for the hour and a half they were gone. On their return we would have dinner around Noon with them and any other family that would show up.

Whether our visits together were at their house or ours, they were always calm, happy and loving. Family is everything. We lost Bubba in 1955 when he had a heart attack and died. I was seven years old and no one thought I was old enough be told he had died and I would never be able to visit him ever again. My first moment of shock and realization that he was gone, was that night when we went to Bubba's house. He was lying in a casket in the parlor dressed in a dark suit, and the house was full of my uncles and aunts crying, talking, drinking and eating. This was my very first introduction to someone dying, and it was meant to be a somber event and conducted with dignity and respect. Bubba was lying there in the casket with his arms folded and his eyes closed. He looked as if he was asleep and could awake at any moment. I wished he would. I was the youngest at the wake because Papa thought I should say goodbye to Bubba while everyone else tried to shelter the younger kids from the fact of life that everyone will die. Since there was alcohol consumed at the wake, the result was the loosening of inhibitions, and many things were said that should not ever be said during the time when only grieving was in order. The subject was always the same: inheritance money. Who deserves it more and how much it will be. Such a shame a scene like that had to play out in front of the group of visitors and family that were there to pay their respects to this fine man. I miss him.

LIFE ON MY BLOCK

Moving into a new house, being new on the block and being a boy had it's challenges. No matter how young or old, short or tall you are, every new boy to the block is scrutinized. Some are accepted and some are not. Unfortunately there isn't an organized body of governing kids from the block that vote to accept you or decide to blackball you from participating in any block activities. Instead there are several small groups of boys of various ages and block status that look you over and either take you in as one of them or pass on you, somewhat like a fraternity. The most favorable scenario is to be accepted by the group of boys that gathered on a porch playing pinochle during their free time. This group was mostly comprised of the older guys that lived on Reinhard Street, and at seventeen, Jerry Cork, was one of the oldest of the boys, and although not Italian was assumed to be the leader of the block.

There was a variety store on one end of the street on the corner where you could purchase most small items you might ever need, except for real food. The name of the store was called by the name of the older woman who owned it and was always there. Her name was Gracie, a woman in her sixties, less than five feet tall, and hunched over a little. Gracie was a Jewish lady with a very strong accent from her mother country Lebanon, and she ruled that little corner store kingdom with an iron hand. Of course the reason she had to oversee the activity in the store as diligently as she did, was due to the number of young hoodlums coming into the store and distracting her long enough to steal anything not nailed down. It was a constant battle, and I felt bad for her trying to fight that losing battle.

The other kind of food she sold that was not "real food" consisted of pretzel sticks, candy, ice cream, and soda pop. Available were most household cleaning supplies, thread, mops, etc. Gracie's was the place where you could buy comic books and star rubber balls. The star rubber balls were a necessity because they were used for playing handball against another boy, by taking turns hitting the ball with your open hand against the building wall after it bounces once on the pavement. The first player to miss the ball's return bounce loses. After playing with the air filled ball in several dozen games, the skin gets worn and thin and then it bursts or splits open. The ball is then cut in half to be used as the ball for stick ball. Stick ball or half ball is played just like baseball. The rules are the same, but the bat is a broom handle cut to size and the ball is a half sphere of the damaged star ball and is pitched underhanded with a variety of expert action by the pitcher. When I wasn't playing half ball in the street with a bunch of the kids, I would join in with other kids at the end of the block overlooking the ongoing pinochle game on the porch of Jerry Cork. It was common to have a dozen onlookers hanging or sitting on the porch railings or standing above the players sitting on the porch deck rails. I was watching and trying to understand the complicated card game. Up to that time WAR was the only card game I knew. After many sessions of observation, I was finally getting a handle on the game. I was slowly getting accepted into the porch group, and therefore automatically accepted into the sub groups on the block.

What does being accepted mean? The main perk was not getting picked on, and the second was being allowed to join in the various games with the other guys.

There was a gang element to living on our block, and if it was found that a boy accepted to be a block member didn't want to be part of anything the block leaders decided, he would be removed from the fold. There wasn't a formal announcement of being a member of the Reinhard Street gang. We didn't have any special jackets or special handshakes. It was more of an unsaid understanding. One important rule stated many times, was that anyone living on Reinhard needed to bypass the neighboring parallel Upland Street when leaving the neighborhood. This action made the destination walk to anywhere much longer, but those living on Upland Street had the same restrictions. Ignoring the restrictions would result in large multi-aged groups of boys colliding on the offending streets' turf with boxing and wrestling type fighting. I never heard of knives or guns being used in these skirmishes so there wasn't the need for law enforcement to be summoned by the neighbors to our neighborhood. I consider myself fortunate that I was never included with any visits to the adjoining street battles due to being one of the youngest of the boys on the block. The older boys were the ones that made the trip to confront our neighbors for trespassing.

Our time living on Reinhard was fun and a real adventure. The thirty minute walk to Catholic school that took me past the large fenced in cemetery off Cobb Creek Parkway presented new experiences for me. The public school was located right across the street from Good Shepard, my Catholic School. So everyone on my street walked to one of the two schools. It was a known fact, at least in my limited knowledge which I learned from the other boys who walked to school with me, that a man known as "Dago" Joe worked at the cemetery. The name "Dago" was one of the unsavory name calling nicknames given to the Italians. I'm not even sure if his name was actually Joe, but that was the name given to the cemetery employee who watched for trespassers, whether they be people or animals. Word was that he was always shooting dogs in the cemetery, and some of the guys said he had taken shots at them just for cutting through the cemetery. I believed everything I heard about him then, but not so much now.

One day going to school, I was walking past the main gate of the cemetery with a couple of my friends when we came upon the bloody scene of a dead dog and three cats. It was difficult to see so early in the morning, but the cause for this crime scene and terrible devastation had our minds whirling as to how this all happened. So we tried to reconstruct the crime. We all settled on "Dago" Joe having shot them all for trespassing in his cemetery. In reality, the more likely cause could be blamed on the dog having rabies and attacking the cats. We will never know the real cause, but the story that went to school and back to the block was the "Dago" Joe version.

The route to school was also the same for going to church since the buildings were connected at the same location. One Sunday walking to church by myself during the middle of the winter there was ice on the sidewalks from a previous storm. I slipped and fell on my side. I got up and realized my arm hurt like Hell but I continued to church keeping the arm at my side. The next forty-five minutes for Mass seemed much longer that day. Afterwards, arriving back home, I changed out of my dress clothes and told Mama and Papa what had happened. They took a quick look at my arm and drove me to the hospital. It turned out the fall I had taken resulted in a compound fracture to my right arm, and I am right-handed. The doctors set my arm and put me in a cast to be worn for the next several weeks. Of course during the next few days I was treated special because I was sort of sick, but in school I didn't get that same treatment. Sister Mary Pachious was my classroom Nun, and despite my having to learn to write with my left hand, she was not willing to tolerate my sloppy handwriting, and noted that discrepancy on every one of the assignments I turned in.

There were special times back on our block too, especially during the time they restricted traffic from our one lane one way street because the city had to dig a deep trench in order to replace old pipes. The project took over a month and caused loads of complaints from the adult residents, but the boys had very different ideas about the inconvenience the trench presented. After the workers finished for the day and left for their homes and our school day was over, we got to play army in the war zone they created for us. We had mounds of dirt, trenches, and equipment, and plenty of soldiers. Life was good!

In the 1950s, we had plenty of deep snowfalls in Philadelphia, and we would get up to ten-foot snow drifts. With schools closed, we were able to construct major fortresses and tunnels. You can imagine the many interlocking complexes built from the kids on the block. Even the snowed in automobiles were used in these forts. When most of the hard work of snow building was completed, it was only natural that snowball fights would follow. The side you were on was the one nearest the fort you had worked on building. The snow ball fights would last for hours. With twenty or so boys on each side, the fights got pretty serious at times, and would sometimes turn into actual fights.

MOM'S FAMILY

My entire world was centered around our street life. We had an A&P grocery store where Mom used to do some of our household shopping, the store was located on Woodland Avenue, which we referred as "The Avenue." The store was about a fifteen minute walk from our house, and halfway there we could stop at my other grandparents' house on Sixty-Third street for lunch with them. This set of grandparents were my mom's Italian family, from Naples, Italy, and they ate their main meal of the day around noon or one o'clock. Usually other members of this large Italian family would also stop by to join the meal. There were sixteen brothers and sisters all living within thirty minutes of my grandparents' house, which was a three-story brownstone with a cellar, and had an adjoining one story storefront. The storefront was owned by my grandparents, and had been used as an Italian Pizza restaurant before I was born. All of the family members worked in the restaurant at times, and I have to believe that the food was fantastic judging from what I ate in my grandmother's kitchen while growing up. Restaurants are universally regarded as one of the hardest businesses to succeed in, and it was not in operation by the time my visits as a child began. We called my grandmother Mama, and she did not speak English, in fact neither did my grandfather, Antonio Barre, which we called Papa, the same as my father.

We always found Mama in the kitchen cooking or baking, unless it was around six o'clock in the evening. That's when the wrestling program on the television would come on. Both of my grandparents absolutely loved the "real" wrestling personalities that they knew and cheered for nightly. Haystacks Calhoun was one of their favorites because of his very large size and the country farmer outfits he wore. During the television wrestling program nobody was allowed to interrupt by talking or moving around, which was weird to me because talking was constant while we visited in the kitchen. Mama was a good sized woman and was always found in a plain day dress with an apron. She was a self-taught master cook that produced a multitude of fine tuned Italian recipes perfected by her over many years. She did not cook before coming to America through Ellis Island in 1918. Her parents' family were very prosperous and that allowed her to live a privileged life in Foggia, Italy. In fact, because of the in house servant staff, she never even brushed her own hair, let alone scrub floors and clean house, until she wed and came to live in America. She did not bring any of the old world recipes with her. Instead her fantastic cooking skills came from remembering how the food tasted growing up, and replicating the recipes and flavors after she came to America and had to cook for her own husband and children.

My grandfather was a slender very well groomed man. His skin tone appeared as if he had a mild tan. His hair was white and thinning, and he kept a well trimmed wisp of a mustache. Around the house he always wore dress pants and a starched white shirt with a sleeveless tee shirt underneath. If he was to go outside for a walk to the avenue to shop, he would add a bow tie to the white shirt, a dress jacket and a white wide brim straw hat to his attire.

On this particular visit to my grandparents' house, Mom and my sisters stayed behind to help prepare the midday meal while I went with Papa shopping. I looked forward to this adventure, but it was a workout since my grandfathers gait was fast and my shorter legs caused me to almost run next to him just to keep up. When we reached the avenue, life was very different, the stores lined both sides of the street, side to side with busy sidewaks with the trolley cars and car traffic in between. Our first stop was the Italian store where we bought a few specialty items we were not able to buy in the regular grocery store. Next stop was down the street to a little hole in the wall store that had cages floor to ceiling on the left wall and glass butcher refrigerator counters all along the right side. The cages had live chickens, rabbits, turkeys, and pigeons. Papa told the butcher which chicken he wanted and the butcher took that chicken into the back of the store to kill, clean and process. The chicken would be brought back to the front and wrapped in white butcher paper. The next store stop was the A&P to buy a couple more small items. By the way, we could have gotten a chicken there also, and probably at a cheaper cost, but buying fresh was the way he always shopped and always would. We headed back to the house for our meal.

Everyone was at Mama's table for the midday meal. The table was full with baskets of Italian bread, a big bowl of pasta with gravy, a separate plate of meatballs, sausage, beef, chicken, and a large bowl of salad. There would be smaller plates of fresh grated parmigiana, a variety of olives, and extra gravy. Also Papa had already made the trip to the cellar to retrieve a couple of bottles of his homemade Chianti styled wine for the meal. Mama only drank a small glass of wine with her meal, and Papa had a couple or so small glasses. Some of the other adult family members who might have showed up would have a glass of wine as well. My mom didn't drink. From the age of seven, Papa made me feel special by pouring me a little red wine into a glass of water, and this ritual continued over the following years until the mix was more wine and less and less water.

The making of the wine was a very important undertaking in my grandfather's house. It happened when the grapes were harvested and available from the wholesalers. His goal was to make enough wine to last for the entire year. The process began with the purchase of fifty crates of wine grapes delivered to the front of his house. Then my uncles helped to stack the crates neatly on the sidewalk until moving them down to the cellar, through the same casement window the coal was delivered through each year. After all of the crates were in the cellar they had to be washed and have the big stems taken off of the wine bunches. When it was ready to do the actual crushing everyone helping was given a job in the process, such as loading the hopper of the large wine grape press. Another person or two would be tasked with turning the metal rod handle located on the top of the press that turned the worm gear to compress the grapes and render the juice out the slatted sides. It was then gathered and poured into the five hundred gallon cask that was laying on its side and was mounted on a strong wooden rack. This process repeated throughout the day and into the night until all of the crates were empty and the last of the grape juice was in the barrel. The work did not end there because they also had a kitchen in the cellar for overflow cooking during the holidays, and clean up had to be done to prevent staining from the grape juice on the counters and floor. The leftover grape skins and seeds also needed to be dealt with. The skins were taken upstairs to Mama to be turned into a candy she made, and Papa took the seeds, pulp, and stems to use in distilling a liquor called Grappa, a clear white liquid that tastes like white lightning, moonshine, or grain alcohol. It is a strong harsh liquor that burns going down your throat; definitely a taste you have to get accustomed to. Nothing went to waste.

Although we ate the major meal in the middle of the day it still lasted close to three hours. My grandparents did not rush their dining, and the meal was over when my grandfather was finished his last bite of food and last sip of wine. The children were fortunate to be excused from the table after we were finished eating, but the adults were trapped and the conversations always continued until the table was cleared.

During the meal everyone was at the table. Once the meal was over the men separated into one corner of the room or stayed at the table and Papa would drag out all of his home made liquors and the delicate miniature serving glasses. Meanwhile the women would proceed to do the kitchen clean up, and prepare to set out the sweets. For the kids it was pretty boring because while the adults were having their discussions and little cups of espresso coffee with liquor drinks, we had to sit on the front enclosed porch and stay quiet. This was the scene for regular weekday and Saturday meals when we visited my grandparents. On Sunday's when the majority of the family was there for dinner the dynamics increased ten fold; more people, more food, and more kids expected to remain quiet. The variety of food Mama prepared on this day was more extensive because Mama wanted to showcase her skills with food. The gravy, or tomato sauce, had the usual meatballs and sausage, but on Sundays because of my Uncle Nick's hunting skills, it was not unusual to find pheasant, deer, rabbit, grouse, or pigeon in the gravy. I can still remember how much we all enjoyed her gravy, and spooning it over different shapes of homemade pastas was delicious.

Mama grew up in the southern part of the Italy and her recipes were influenced by what she ate. She didn't cook while growing up, and the live-in house chef cooked all of the meals, so the recipes she prepared were southern Italy style also. Many of those dishes she put together were made with various greens and vegetables, and always with great olive oil. The main difference in Southern cuisine and Northern cuisine is that the southern part of Italy cooks more green vegetables and uses olive oil, whereas the Northern Italy cooks have more meat dishes and use butter.

Differences in the way the southern Italians and the northern Italians cooked wasn't the only distinction between the Italians. For example, I observed that my father was never at any of my Moms family meals at Mama's. The excuse usually given was that he was working. But that wasn't a good explanation for Sunday's dinners. He had plenty of time to join us after he took his mom to church. It was years later that I heard it was because neither side of the family accepted the other sides of the families, each thought they were more important than the other only because they came from different regions of Italy and each thought they were the only true Italians. The Sicilian side didn't recognize or for that matter even care for the Naples Italians and vice versa. Thankfully my parents marriage and their children kept both sides calm by acting as if they liked each other, or at least tolerant and civil toward the other side of the family. Throughout my early years that was how it was, and it worked because there was never a declaration announcing a vendetta between the two families. This situation was not unique in our two large families. There were other marriages that caused riffs due to marrying outside of their towns and provinces.

In Italy every region is separated by hills and valleys which makes each area it's own world. Most Italians born in their hilltop towns never venture out of the town. They are born and die in the same house their families had lived in for generations. All of their family and friends know everyone in the town where they live and work, and anyone outside of their world is a stranger and can't possibly be as important as they are. A very small and closed minded approach to not accepting someone for no other reason than where their families came from. But that was how it was.

SELF-EMPLOYMENT

Growing up on my street block, gave me the opportunity to earn some easy money by taking my wagon around to the neighbors and asking for old newspapers they were finished with that I could have. Many neighbors gave me their old papers and when I had the wagon loaded beyond the point it was easy to pull, me and one of my friends headed to the junk shop up on the Avenue. At the junk shop a rough looking individual in charge weighed the loaded wagon and wrote the number on his pad, then unloaded the wagon and weighed it again, writing down that number also. He then did the math with weight times cost per pound and paid me. This scenario played out several times until one day a neighbor also gave me some copper pipe with the newspaper so I slipped it in between the newspapers on the wagon. I thought this was going to be great since the copper weighed so much more than newspaper I would get more money. Sure enough when the junk yard guy unloaded the newspapers he saw the copper pipe, but didn't say anything and paid us for the full weight of the wagon. It wasn't until years later I discovered when I was trying to pull a scam over on the junk yard with the extra weight of the copper pipe, he took advantage of me and paid the lower price for the newspaper and hidden pipe. The price for the copper pipe fetched a much higher price than the newspaper. A lesson well learned.

Up on the Avenue among all the stores there were two movie theaters, the "Ben" and the "Benson," and they were located within two blocks of each other on the same side of the street. The theaters had been there from the beginning of the movie industry. During World War Two the movies provided the public news of the war progress overseas for the Allies by way of the newsreels played before each movie feature. My Mamma went to watch movies at these theaters even though she wasn't able to understand the language. It didn't matter; she wasn't there to see the movie for the nickel admission price, she went to get the promotion gift they were giving to promote attendance. After many of these movie visits she had a whole set of glassware that was later know as carnival glass.

Years later I went to the same movie theaters with a couple of the kids from the block that my mom approved of. I felt pretty grown up being allowed to be up on the Avenue at the movies at the age of eleven without any adult supervision. This freedom occurred only a few times, but those few times were great. Nothing ever went wrong to restrict me from going to the movies more often. It was just that my family didn't have the extra cash to allow me to go to the movies, despite the low admission fee.

There was only one confrontation I encountered up on the Avenue after leaving an afternoon matinee one Saturday at the Benson Theater. I was with one of my friends from the block and a couple of kids approached us and one of them got in my face. He said he wanted the hair comb that was in my back pocket. As insignificant as a used comb was, I still didn't want to give it up to him. He was about my age and size and he started to grab for the comb. I pushed him off and we started to fist fight. Fortunately, neither my friends nor his friend jumped into the fight; they were just watching and cheering for their fighter. After several minutes I must have be able to get in a lucky punch that made my opponent give up the fight and run down the street. Looking back at the event it really wasn't much of a fight, but the news and embellished story that went back to the block gave everyone a subject to talk about for days to come.

TOUGH TIMES

There were good times and there were hard times. The toughest times were during the winter when work was hard to find. My father's occupation was a union plasterer and when there was work, it was plentiful. I remember one Friday when Papa came home from work and he slapped three one hundred dollar bills on the kitchen table where we were eating dinner. I'm sure he was proud of how much he had made, and it made us all stare at the bills in awe. We had never seen a bill larger than a twenty. In 1955 that was a small fortune, but he didn't have the opportunity to always earn that kind of money. Being able to budget a paycheck was the hardest task a family had to do, and many failed at it because there wasn't enough money to allow for any margin of error. My family fell short of making ends meet many times, especially during the winter when jobs were scarce and layoffs were not. We experienced utilities being turned off at times, and not having any money to buy food. Both of my parents could go to their parents and ask for short term help, but since they were both very independent and proud, they never did.

I recall one winter with the electric cut off, I was upstairs in my bedroom wearing my winter snow coat, playing with the Lionel train set I had set up on a piece of plywood. Not having electricity, I was pushing the train cars around the tracks playing the only way I could. After awhile it too went beyond being fun due to the cold, so I just crawled into bed still in my coat and got under the covers until morning. Times were tough, and childhood was an innocent time of life. I thought everything was normal and that was how everyone lived. I never had a thought back then that we were poor and had less than other people.

Dinners during these tough times were different also. Hunger was felt by all, and the children were always the first to get the food portions we had. My parents would get whatever was left, if anything. One particular dinner I remember consisted of a slice of bread with mustard on it, we were still hungry but there was nothing else to eat. I'm sure this broke my parents hearts. The good thing about these perceived hardships was as kids we didn't know any different, as we didn't have any other lifestyle to compare to. As far as we knew, how we lived was normal, and experiencing the highs and lows, and a feast or famine lifestyle was how life was meant to be. I believe this was healthy for us because we did not judge or condemn our parents for not providing us a better life. The fact is Papa had many opportunities to earn more money with my mom's brothers who had associations with the Mafia. They offered many times to take him in because he was a Sicilian, and he would be readily accepted. He turned them down each time. He refused to go down that road as hard as it must have been for him to see us not living as well as the rest of the family. My uncles kept their illegal business dealings among themselves, so neither my grandparents nor my other aunts and uncles knew the extent of their involvement with the mob.

In reality living through the hardships of that time in my life made everything in my future much better. You have to feel the pain of being without before you can achieve the feeling of gain. As hard as it seemed back then, the good times easily outnumbered the hard times.

JERSEY FAMILY VISITS

One of good times I recall pertained to our visits to New Jersey to visit relatives from Mom's side of the family. Aunt Lizzy and Uncle Rex had a nice house there and a vacation house in Hollywood, Florida. They owned a restaurant named "Rexy's" located on the Black Horse Parkway just north of the Philadelphia line. When we visited them it was usually at the restaurant since they were always there working in the business. We were always happy to be treated to their great tasting Italian food, especially the meatballs.

Aunt Sarah and Uncle Frank lived in Jersey close to Aunt Lizzy. They raised some chickens and had a large fig tree in their backyard. Uncle Frank drove a tractor trailer truck moving produce around New Jersey. Up to then I had only seen live chickens in cages at the butchers located on Woodland Avenue in Philadelphia. I had no idea how much work was necessary daily to grow a little chick into a full sized eatable chicken. The daily feeding was one task, but cleaning their house, replenishing the straw, and maintaining the chickens health took time and effort. Also controlling the field rats who were always trying to get to the chicken feed, and preventing predators from eating the chickens before you got the chance to, was a very difficult task. But if you succeed, the rewards are fresh eggs and the tastiest chicken you will ever eat.

On these visits, as with other family visits, once we got

around the dinner table in a relative's house or my uncle's restaurant, all children were expected to behave and be quiet, at least during the meal. Again, after the children finished their meals, they were dismissed from the table and sent to an area that would not bother the adults for the next couple of hours. This is what all of the kids expected since it happened at each and every gathering, but it wasn't a bad thing. These were the times when we learned things about how other kids of various ages around the Philadelphia region were living their lives. Things such as what music was being listened to, how to act with a girl or boy you may really like, and other important knowledge on various topics one needed to know in the maturing process. My cousins on both sides of the family truly enriched my worldly knowledge. I was like a sponge absorbing all of the enlightening information shared by my older cousins, both boys and girls. Learning what my older cousins knew propelled me beyond my years by knowing a little bit more than others on the block my age. Besides finding out information pertaining to growing up and being cool, we also shared things about our parents and various relatives as overheard by my cousins. Information or rumors such as my uncle Salvatore, on my fathers side of the family, was connected with the Mafia. This must have been true since many of my cousins had heard the same and decided this was a fact. Years later I found out this was true, and there were other members of the family on both sides connected as well. But even when I found that out, I did not associate being connected with the Mafia as being bad or illegal. It was just an Italian thing, like belonging to a club.

After seeing my cousins at the Jersey gathering and learning more about boys and girls, and finding out about that thing that is done between a man and a woman to have a baby, which was hard to believe, I gained a new insight to an entire new area of life for me. My thoughts from that point in time were full of this recently learned knowledge about girls and boys intimate relationships. Even at my age I started looking for any opportunity to get closer to a girl and maybe even try the things I had only heard of. At that family gathering I learned the "facts of life."

The difficulty I faced was two fold. One of the hurdles was that I was Catholic, went to Catholic church and went to Catholic school. The other hurdle had to do with one of the Ten Commandments that pertained to me, the one preached "NO INTERCOURSE UNTIL MARRIED." That might not be the actual commandment, or the exact wording, but that was what all of the Catholics were taught. This presented me with quite a dilemma. I wanted to get intimate with a girl, but was not allowed, so for the time being I would keep my desires for girls to myself and confined to my thoughts and only my thoughts.

For the person that never attended Catholic school there weren't that many differences from public school. The teachers were Nuns and Priests were the vice principal and principals. Prayer was part of the curriculum along with daily Mass in the adjoining church. There was a crucifix with Jesus on the front wall above the blackboards and examples of upper and lower case cursive letters positioned above the blackboard to use as a guide in learning to write. The nuns were allowed, and in some cases, expected to administer discipline. The discipline was in many forms, but the one method used most often was the yardstick to rap the misbehaving students across the knuckles or back.

My school nun, Sister Mary Pachious, had a unique way of always having the yardstick with her by slipping it through one sleeve up to her shoulder. It stuck out of the sleeve but wasn't that noticeable until she whipped it out to crack you on the back. It was very effective.

THE MARYLAND MOVE

In 1961 my parents were convinced to leave Philadelphia and move to the suburbs of Washington, DC in Maryland to join several of my mom's side of the family for work. My uncle Joe was building a large housing development on property that was previously woodland, and he had the idea that having family working for him would provide him with the best supervision for the building project. So he sold two of the built houses to two of my uncles, and gave a house to his parents, and my grandparents, and provided a house for us to live in, for as long as it remained on the market for sale. We were the only part of the family that didn't have the money to purchase a house at any price since my parents lost the house on Reinhard Street in Philly to foreclosure. With no work they were not able to keep up the mortgage payments in the winter. During the winter months work for the trades really dried up, especially for the plasterers. Individuals in the trade had to budget their money during times when work was plentiful. There was a lot of overtime, and by budgeting they were able to live normally during the lean times. Unfortunately Papa wasn't in that camp. He was a day-to-day person. When times were flush with cash from his paychecks, things were real good, but when work got slow again, our family suffered. To get by, he would never go to the family for a handout or short term loan, nor would he go on assistance or unemployment because of his pride.

There was one time I remember my mom going behind his back during a particularly low time in our lives while in Philly and asked one of my uncles for money to buy food for us kids. When Papa found out he exploded and stormed out of the house and didn't return for a couple of hours. When he did return he slammed a stack of bills on the kitchen table and told mom to return the money to my uncle then grabbed a beer and left the room. I never heard where the money had come from but I was sure it wasn't from working because it was night time and he was only gone for a couple of hours.

Now that I know more, my guess is that he got the money from a loan shark. Loan sharks lend money to those people that can't get a bank loan, which does fill a gap in the system. But the downside is that the interest rate for the loan can be set anywhere, usually around three times the normal bank rates. If you default on a bank loan they foreclose or take back collateral from you and your credit rating drops which prevents you from getting another loan from another lending institution. If you default on a loan shark, or fall behind on payments, your collateral is your body, and therefore your body is beaten; how badly depends on the loan size. A default on a large loan could possibly cost you your life.

Even though we were only living in one of my uncles houses on a temporary basis, my sisters and myself still had to enroll in schools which we did, and that was a different experience right from the start. In the mornings we would walk up to the intersecting street with a bunch of other kids and board different yellow buses heading to various schools. My bus ride destination was to a public Junior High School, and when the bus stopped and emptied, we stood around outside with a couple of hundred other kids until a bell rang.

Then we all went inside at the same time into a cafeteria/ assembly room. From there we looked on a wall of notebook papers with lists of names for the classes and rooms we were required to report to.

After the first day of orientation, it became school as I knew it, except with all of the new students I did not know, and a couple of cute girls that smiled and looked at me whenever we passed in the halls. It seems that the thoughts I kept contained in my mind of what boys and girls can do are no longer confined. I really want to get closer to these girls.

THE GIRLFRIEND EXPERIENCE

As it turns out getting closer to girls wasn't as easy as I thought it might be, and those couple of cute girls I thought I would pursue didn't want anything to do with me. My first girlfriend experience happened after learning which girls had the reputation of being loose with their sexual practices. Janice was this type of girl, and I called her my girlfriend after only being with her for three days. After going to the movies and making out and feeling her breasts, we sort of had sex, the first time for me. She got on the floor in front of my seat, unzipped my fly, removed my penis and put it in her mouth. Soon after she got started it was finished. I had been very excited so it didn't take long, but it was the greatest feeling I had ever felt. When we walked out of the movie theater I felt as if I was on top of the world. She, on the other hand, said we should break up. That was the end of my three day relationship. The short relationship was troubling to me but not even close to what I knew I had to face: Confession.

I had to confess to a priest the following Saturday and tell him of the sinful event that I was part of in the movie theater. If I didn't do that I wasn't able to receive communion at Mass on Sunday, and then my parents would know I committed some awful sin. After going to confession, doing my penance of twenty Our Father's and twenty Hail Mary's, and surviving that anguish, I decided to clean up my act.

So after the short relationship with Janice I thought I should change my love life tactics by not pursuing the loose girls with bad reputations. Instead I would seek out the girls that went to Our Lady of Mercy Catholic girls school. Talking among the guys I hung with at school and on my street block, it was decided that the girls who went to that school either became a Nun or a Prostitute. Of course this wasn't a true statement, but teenage boys tend to hold onto the perceptions they come up with, true or not, especially when getting support from your friends.

I did date a few girls that went to Our Lady of Mercy, and I am positive none of them had a chance of becoming a Nun. One Irish girl named Ciara was a scholar in school, a real beauty, and fully developed with a great shape. Ciara's dad was a doctor, who owned his own General Practice with an office in their neighborhood community about six miles away from where I lived. In order for me to see her after school I would have to walk or hitchhike to her apartment. I had a drivers license, but I didn't have a car, and Papa would never let me borrow his car.

We lived in an apartment because we had to. All seven of us jammed into a two bedroom apartment with my parents in one room, my four sisters in the other, and I had the couch located in the dining room that doubled as my bed. I'm not complaining about the close quarters because when you are a kid you get used to whatever the conditions are around you and accept it as normal. It's when you get a little older that you start comparing your lifestyle with that of your friends.

Ciara's family lived in an apartment instead of a house because her father was a busy doctor and he didn't have the time or desire to maintain a house, yard, and any necessary repairs. They rented an upscale newer three bedroom garden apartment for the four members of their family. Their place was decorated with all new furnishings, at least that was how I perceived it. Ciara invited me for dinner a few times because I was usually at her house visiting her after school. Those dinners usually featured enormous steaks, potatoes, and string beans. I was never sure if her dad was showing off his success, or if they ate that way all of the time. Whatever the case, I looked forward to being invited to join them for dinner. I never had her to dinner at our house and I never would invite her, as the meals were completely opposite from hers. My mom planned our meals with a lot of thought given to them, the meals had to taste good, they had to be nutritious, and most of all affordable. Not a hard feat with Italian style cooking.

My mother was an excellent Italian cook and had a multitude of recipes in her mind's cookbook. But pasta and meatballs in her tomato gravy, or Chicken Cacciatore with pasta or potatoes with iceberg lettuce salad found the way to our table for most of the meals because of the ability to stretch the meal at a lower cost. The fact is none of us actually gave a second thought about the meal plans. We all loved the food and there weren't that many nightly meals where we didn't have a friend or two of mine or friends of my sisters join us for dinner. There was always enough pasta to share.

In those days everyone was required to be at the evening meal table, but this isn't what I found to be the case at some of my friends houses. In their homes the evening meal was eaten whenever the family members got home. They would eat in front of the television in the living room, or alone at the dining room table. I liked the way our family recited the dinner prayer, and discussed family business. We had the evening meal and shared the daily events.

I wanted to participate in sports at school but was unable since I didn't have a car to drive home after practices. So instead, I went up to the Boys Club close to my house and signed up for the boxing program. I had never boxed and had only been in one fistfight, but I immediately took to this sport and it turned out I was good at it. The club trainer, Gus, had been a prize fighter in his day and remembered enough to share his knowledge with us new want-to-be-fighters. In the rink we fought against other boys that weighed about the same, that is, in our weight class, and we competed against other clubs that had boxing programs. After only a year I was top contender in my weight class in Golden Gloves. Gus said I was a natural and had promise. I didn't stay with the boxing game though. I was preoccupied at the time with girls, and I spent my time engaging in that sport instead.

HIGH SCHOOL - CRIME 101

During the following years I often wondered why anyone would want to belong or be associated with the Mafia since everything I ever heard was that there were a lot of mob hits and the Mafia was on the other side of the law. There had to be a money element advantage otherwise why would anyone risk the possible downside in being a member. I would struggle with this question for the next few years while making my way through high school.

High school for me consumed too many hours, days and years. Not that I wasn't interested in school. I learned easily without much effort and I think that was the reason it didn't hold my interest. Not having to work too hard at grasping the lessons gave me the opportunity to spend time and efforts on other endeavors, such as finding ways to make quick money. So at night when other schoolmates were at home studying and doing homework, I was out of the house as soon as dinner was over, under the guise of going to the library or a friends house to study. In reality I had hooked up with a guy named Marco that worked in the kitchen of Leo's restaurant located on Chester Avenue. He ran a small numbers game for the neighborhood. The numbers game was betting three numbers for each day for any amount you wanted to bet. The winning numbers were based on the last three digits of the amount race track bettors placed on race day at a major racetrack that was printed in racing journals and major newspapers in New York. This was illegal and deemed a racket, but I was able to make some extra cash by picking up little pieces of paper with the bet money from the neighborhood betting participants and returning the transactions to Marco. If there were any winners the following day, I would bring the calculated monies to the winner, usually providing me with tip money and a new bet. Life was good, so good that I had to be really careful as to how I spent my new found wealth. I couldn't disclose to anyone what I was doing.

It was frustrating not sharing my lucrative side job, but silence would set the tone for the rest of my future illegal endeavors.

I did make mistakes though. Once while skipping school and making slip pickups in the north end of my territory, I ran across a group of thugs that apparently needed the paper bag of cash I was carrying more than Marco did. After confronting me and demanding the bag I turned to run but didn't get more than two steps when all three began to wail on me, even after they had the bag. That lesson cost me lots of black and blue bruises and a few cuts above my eyes and nose. Not as bad as it could have been considering I had no broken bones, stab wounds, or gunshots, and I didn't die.

The two worse things that happened beyond the injuries was that Marco wasn't at all happy about the mugging, not because of me getting beat up, but that he had to cover the losses with the winning customers. Thankfully no one hit the number big that he would have had to cover, or else he probably would have shot me.

The other thing that happened was going back to school the following day. Even though I had Papa and Mom convinced I had gotten into a fight with a kid from school, and told them I had won, when I got into class the Nun sent me to the office to see Father O'Leary. My Nun teacher had already reported to Father O'Leary that I missed school the day before and did not bring an excuse slip to class. When called into Father O'Leary's office he didn't even look up for several minutes, trying to make me sweat, and he did. Finally he looked up and a surprised expression appeared on his face when he saw my busted up face across the desk from him. Without initially commenting he just started nodding his head as if he new the whole story already. It should be understood that a Catholic priest in a city neighborhood knows an abundance of information from simple observations and of course the confessions he hears from parishioners spewing out their worse sins. When Father O'Leary finally spoke he said "Tony, how long did you think you would get away with skipping school and breaking the law". I was shocked so badly I couldn't initially respond, but when I did all I could say was that I was sorry. After that I pretty much just listened to his lecture which ended with 'Tony, I want you to bring your parents to school for a meeting tomorrow morning". That was much worse than getting pounded in the alley by the thugs. Having to tell Papa was one thing, he would just bust on me, but mom would play the "how I disappointed her" card which would bring the tears and the anticipated restrictions to my activities.

After the school conference about skipping school, and the realization that their son was running numbers, the following drama, and multiple punishments given to me included the demand to stop working for Marco. I went back to school and buckled down to studies.

After three weeks I got restless and I found myself hooked up with Marco again and he introduced me to a guy named Aldo that ran a few other innovative businesses in addition to the numbers racket. In reality Aldo turned out to be the next tier boss that Marco delivered his numbers proceeds to, and had to answer to if the business failed to deliver at the expected levels.

Aldo had several underlings such as Marco all delivering large sums of cash that couldn't be easily run through a legitimate banking institution. For that reason Aldo had his hands in a number of businesses that routinely accepted cash as payment for various services. He owned a bar, a restaurant, and dry cleaners, and all were used to hide the cash from the numbers operation. These businesses would make many small deposits with the illegal cash, then find various innovative ways to pay Aldo for services or products he never performed or delivered. This was how the cash was washed or laundered.

The numbers racket was very lucrative but it wasn't the only cash cow he had coming in. He was also running a drug business selling marijuana and prescription drugs. This business was generating more than any of the others and was growing fast. Aldo was doing very well for himself, but he too had to answer to someone up the line that was even more powerful and connected than himself. He was connected with the Mafia, also known as the Cosa Nostra by its members, so that means I was associated with the Mafia at the lowest level through Aldo and Marco. I remember thinking about my position in this multilevel power ladder and actually felt a little proud of breaking the law with a Mafia connection, kind of crazy and strange, and not at all healthy.

But that's how I felt.

I had four more months of high school prior to graduation, and I had already decided not to go to college. I was making good money with the ability to triple my income if I didn't have to attend school. So I asked Aldo for additional tasks to increase my income and he complied by making me a dealer for the marijuana and drug sales.

LEARNING THE BUSINESS

It turns out that selling illegal drugs wasn't that difficult for me. The customer base was already there and was growing quickly by word of mouth. I would take the call from the customer, inform them of the price for the product, then go to my source for the product and pay the negotiated price we had previously agreed upon. I delivered the product to the customer after counting their purchase money, and beat feet out of there. The hardest part was handling much larger sums of money. So I acquired a 38 caliber short barrel Smith and Weston hand gun to prevent thugs from robbing and beating me again like years ago. That was my solution for the earlier lesson. It was business as usual without any hitches for months and I was raking in the cash. I didn't want for anything and I was partying like a rock star. I was having a blast, still living at home with my parents and sisters, driving a new Cadillac, and buying presents for my family. My family suspected I was up to no good, but with the presents and treats coming in regularly, they all just turned their heads and stopped asking questions.

One cold February night I was meeting with a new customer referred to me from a long time customer of various types of pills. The meeting was to be in front of the corner drug store. How appropriate right? I usually showed up to meeting sites at least fifteen minutes early in order to case the area and see if it was safe for me, and for this meeting everything seemed in order. The new customer showed up on time and walked towards me at the front of the store. When we were face to face he identified himself and pulled a fistful of money out of his pocket asking me if I had the pills, and I said I did. He said he wasn't giving the money until he saw the pills, I told him that wasn't the way this business was done, but he insisted on seeing the goods first. Unfortunately I complied.

At that moment a badge came out of the customers pocket and two other men appeared from the darkness with guns drawn. I was screwed.

Next I was face down on the sidewalk arms above my head handcuffed, my gun was found and taken with my pill stash on me and the rest that they found after searching my car. At the police station I was thrown into jail after two hours of questioning. They got no information from me. The following day I saw the judge and was thrown back into jail until the court date two weeks from then. When the court trial finally happened it was an airtight case for the State of Pennsylvania, the verdict was Guilty. I was given one year in prison for drug dealing and carrying an unlicensed hand gun. A gigantic disappointment and embarrassment for my family, and I lost one year of my life.

My daily life in prison was very routine. I read a lot and lifted weights in order to bulk up. Other than the three meals per day, and exercise in the yard, I talked with the other inmates learning about their crimes and their money schemes on the outside. I was fortunate enough not to get any sexual advances or pressure from the inmate population like others had to go through. I was let out of prison after nine months and I headed home to a not-too-welcoming homecoming.

After I was jailed the neighbors treated my family differently, and my family treated me as what I had become – the black sheep of the family. For an Italian this pill was harder to swallow than the ones I sold that got me to this place in life. I was always told the Family was everything and it always came first. I didn't feel I went against the family, it was just an unfortunate instance of not taking enough caution with my business dealings. That won't happen again.

ATLANTIC CITY MOVE

I still had money hidden away and I thought a new start would be in order for me. I told my parents I was moving so that I could stay out of trouble. I would still have to act like I lived at home because I needed to check in with my parole officer for the next three months. But I was actually going to find a place to live in Atlantic City, New Jersey. It was close to home but not too close, just the right distance away to start a new life. I found a small two bedroom apartment above Mario's Pizza located off Atlantic Avenue on South Georgia Street. Finding the apartment so quickly was lucky, and the job that I landed was working in the Pizza place downstairs. It was perfect since Mario was going to give me a break on the rent as an employee.

Making pizza was fine and I was making money, but nowhere near the amount of money I was making before going into the slammer, so I needed to get something going, and it would be pills. While working in the shop making and selling pizzas I identified several individuals who would most likely know drug dealers in the neighborhood. The difficulty was getting them to divulge their knowledge. I began asking those certain individuals if they knew of anyone that could get me some uppers, a stimulant that gives increased confidence, mood, energy and awareness. My contact information came pretty quickly, only after the third person I asked. All I had to do then was a little leg work, and I was meeting with a link to the neighborhood drug distributor.

I met Gabriele in the rear of the laundromat located around the block from the pizza joint under the pretense of wanting to buy drugs. Instead, within a few minutes I was negotiating a deal to work for him citing my qualifications and experience from doing similar work in Philadelphia. Gabriele said he would let me know later when he came by the pizza shop that evening. Later that night towards closing I still hadn't heard from Gabriele and thought I would have to continue the search for a way into the drug scene, when three guys came in the shop. These guys didn't appear to be the type who would be picking up pizza to bring home for the wife and kids. Rather they looked like the menacing type that would pull guns and rob the joint. I asked if I could help them and they responded with a question, "Are you Tony?" I responded with a yes, and the oldest of the men said his name was Enzo and told me to lock the front door. After complying I sat down with him while the other two men stood, one by the door and the other constantly watching my every move. Enzo said he checked with his contacts in Philadelphia about me and found the feedback favorable, and that I hadn't had any dealings with drugs since I got out of the slammer. I nodded in agreement. He told me Gabriele worked for him and that he had twelve others doing the same sales throughout Atlantic City. He wanted me to oversee the thirteen dealers and answer directly to him. He laid out the perks of the position, and talked briefly about the drawbacks and dangers. I focused primarily on the benefits, especially the outrageous money I would be making, I dismissed the drawbacks of arrest or death. Anyway Enzo and I shook hands binding our contract agreement.

JOHNNY RINZO

I kept my job at the pizza parlor and my apartment upstairs because I was determined not to make the same mistakes that ended up with me doing time in prison. I wanted to keep a very low profile and go beyond caution to keep me from being directly connected to any of my illegal dealings. So the first thing I needed to find was someone I could rely upon, but most importantly I needed to find someone I could trust and act as a buffer between me and the dealers just like Enzo was doing by hiring me. The guy I kept going back to in my mind was Johnny Rinzo from my old neighborhood in Philly. Johnny was only half Italian with his dad being Irish and his mom a Sicilian, but his heart was all Italian and we had been friends for years. But would he make the move to Atlantic City? I didn't know because we had lost touch with each other after I got arrested, and at that time he was still running slips for the numbers game with Marco. I wasn't sure if he would take the chance to move up to the drug racket that had more chances for undesirable consequences. I gave him a call and asked him if we could meet in Cherry Hill, New Jersey for lunch and a talk, and he said yes. When I saw him it was like we had been together the prior day instead of the eighteen months since. After we got our Hoagies, which were a combination of Italian meats and cheeses with a pepper relish on an Italian bread roll, we went back to my car to eat them. Once in the car I didn't waste any time getting down to business. He started on the hoagie while I did the talking. I laid out my whole plan for him to be an overseer of the thirteen dealers in my organization and he would answer to me only. When we finished our Hoagies I asked him what he thought and if he had any questions and his response was simply "No, I'm in."

Johnny Rinzo was a quiet fellow that stood six feet, four inches and was built like a football player due to his daily routine of working out with weights. He also carried a pistol that I only presumed he knew how to use, because I was never with him when he had to use it. We got along quite well since we thought a lot alike, and anticipated what the other's next move would be. That saved time and the need for explanations.

A few days later Johnny brought his stuff to my apartment and took over the second bedroom until he could find a place of his own. Living with me was not an option, he couldn't live with me since my mode of operation was to maintain a wall of separation between myself and those I do business with, and I was determined to stick to my own rule.

Over the following days Johnny and I were meeting with all of the thirteen dealers individually in order to learn about their territories and how they handled themselves while conducting business. I needed to get a feel for which ones would go along with this new pecking order change Enzo had put in place. For the most part the dealers, at least verbally, were agreeable, but I detected the mannerisms and body language of two of the dealers that gave me a bad feeling. I thought at some point down the road there would be trouble with them. There wasn't anything conclusive that I could put my finger on, but I made a mental note to watch them carefully.

Within a few weeks I had Johnny and his dealer crew of thirteen operating at full capacity and the money was flowing in three hundred times more than my Philly business ever brought in. Enzo should have been pleased, and he was. Enzo and I were making large money and taking the least risks of everyone involved. After several months of operation with business doubling and piles of cash passing through our counting rooms daily, everything was running smoothly. And then it wasn't.

PROVIDING AN EXAMPLE

While going over the books and comparing territory spreadsheets among the thirteen dealers, there was an income stream pattern change that occurred five weeks after I took over. Two of the East Side territory routes had a distinct income dip that has never returned to its previous normal level. It just happened that both territories were run by the two dealers I had the bad feeling about, and this is the trouble I anticipated was going to occur; stealing from me and Enzo.

The following day I had Johnny meet with one of the thieving dealers. I had instructed him to accompany the dealer on each number slip pickup for the next four days, then I would compare the income with the previous weeks income. Whatever the outcome of the unique audit will probably apply to the other thieving dealer, and will be dealt with accordingly. I told Johnny if the dealer had any questions about this to tell him I was having you do a ride along with each of the other dealers to better familiarize ourselves with the customers and territories. Nothing else needs to be said.

After Johnny concluded the four day ride along with the dealer, I went over the proceeds carefully and the result was that all of a sudden the income level for each of the day's take had jumped back to the level just before the discovered dip in income. So we have two thieves that have to be dealt with, but how severely? An example would have to be made of them to prevent others thinking they might get away with stealing from me.

I called Johnny at his new apartment down the block and instructed him to bring me the dealer thieves in the morning, and also to have our enforcers Rocco and Luca, here as I have a job for them.

All of the players showed up as expected and I began my interview with each dealer separately in a different room. I asked him if he knew the dealer in the other room was skimming money from the numbers proceeds. His answer at first was no, but when I told him the other dealer had pointed the finger at him for stealing and said it was his idea, he immediately blurted out it was the other dealer's idea. I then asked if they still had the money to repay the stolen funds, and he said they had some of it. I told Johnny to take him out of the room and send in the other dealer. I went through the exact line of questioning and the answers came back the same way, except this dealer said he still had most of the stolen money. Johnny took this dealer out of the room and sat him next to the other one. I told them that Rocco and Luca would take each dealer to the place the remainder of the stolen money was stashed, then turn it over to Rocco and Luca. They got up and left to follow my orders. Unknown to the dealers, after they delivered whatever monies they have to Rocco and Luca, they both would be beaten very badly, but not killed. And their territories would be divided and serviced by the remaining eleven dealers until a replacement could be found. That is the measured example I sent to deter stealing from me in the future.

TIERS OF POWER

Angelo Bruno was the head of the Family for the Philadelphia and South Jersey areas, which included Atlantic City. Enoch "Nocky" Johnson was the first to make Atlantic City his crime empire through bribery and strong arm methods. Being the head of a family in a territory that brings in substantial revenue automatically made him a target for other Family heads that wanted that lucrative income and were willing to do anything to take control of that family and territory, usually by a hit on the boss. That is how Angelo Bruno ascended to power as did the Family heads before him. The boss I answered to was Enzo and the boss he answered to was the head of the Family Angelo Bruno. That was the ladder structure of power until recently. Word on the street announced that Enzo had been disposed of after being found pocketing a couple of hundred thousand dollars that should have been sent up the line to the coffers of Angelo Bruno. Seemed to me stealing happened at every level and examples had to be made when that occured to discourage it happening again. Word came down through channels I would now be answering to Salvatore Cosa as my immediate boss. Salvatore came up through the Philly area territory so he was not as familiar as I was with Atlantic City. I was a little pissed Bruno didn't elevate me into Enzo's position, but it isn't a democratic system: you don't get a vote.

Less than eight months later Bruno was murdered by

his own consigliere (Italian for advisor) Antonio Caponigro, who in turn was ordered killed by the Commission for acting without permission. Philip Testa rose to the Family head in place of Bruno and immediately started to clean house after uncovering a coup which was planned to take out Bruno. Involved in this coup was Enzo's replacement, Salvatore Cosa, that was said to have grand ambitions to take over Atlantic City by overthrowing Bruno and his close followers. Even if this revelation was not true or accurate, it made sense. So he was eliminated, just that easy. With Salvatore gone Testa put me in his slot and I would now answer directly to him. In turn I gave Johnny more responsibility, and he chose a guy under him to take care of the everyday smaller details.

Now that I was in a more prestigious position, and had more control and power, it was even more necessary to watch my back and be sure of my actions than before. I have seen how easy it is to get whacked and I wasn't going that way.

The new position expanded my income stream drastically since the numbers game had been the predominate focus I controlled. But now bookmaking, money laundering, prostitution, and illegal gambling played a much larger portion of my oversight description. I had been nibbling at all of these sectors ever since I came to Atlantic city, but now I had to find or identify individuals that would be responsible for the day-to-day activities in each of those businesses and then have them answer to me as Johnny does for the numbers business.

After only three years since I made my move to Atlantic City, I have been able to accumulate a lot of real estate around the small apartment which I now own and still live in above the pizza shop. Other properties include the laundromat around the corner on South Georgia Avenue, and Mario's Restaurant on Arkansas Avenue. All were bought with the vast amount of cash I was taking in that wasn't part of the required percentage to send up the line to the boss. Real Estate was the easiest method to wash vast amounts of cash, so I would buy any and all property, no matter what condition, that came on the market, or that I heard might be available for sale. I was paying cash for each of them.

In addition to my core properties, I bought any low value wreck of a house or apartment building that went on the market. If I wanted a property that wasn't for sale, I exerted pressure and forced a buyout of the owner. The protection insurance arm of my organization produced a very strong stream of cash. We would go to the business owner whether it was a candy store, gas station or restaurant and sell them insurance to protect against non-family connected thugs robbing their stores and protect them from being mugged there. The threat was real, so that made the insurance necessary. Besides, if the store owner decided not to buy the insurance, the store would be robbed and the owners would be beaten by us therefore everyone bought the insurance which was collected weekly by my men.

As time went by, the occurrence of having to make examples of members in my organization became more frequent, as expected, because of the sizable amount of cash coming in from every direction. Everyone that observed the flow of that much money wanted a larger piece, or all of the action. Violent street skirmishes were a regular occurrence and the spots at the top were becoming hazardous to hold. After Angelo Bruno was murdered, Testa took over and promoted me to my present position last year. After only one year as

Family boss, he too was killed from a vengeance hit relating to Bruno's murder.

The man to become the Family head was Nicky "Little Nicky" Scarfo, five feet, five inches tall, with a terrible short fuse and an outrageous temper. He enjoyed using brutal measures in conducting his business, so you didn't want to be on the wrong side of this guy.

At this time there wasn't any physical change to my operation except for the name of the man at the top to whom we forwarded the money. In Scarfo's eyes I'm sure he considered me somewhat of a threat to him because I had control of all of the businesses in Atlantic City, and all of the manpower, which meant I also had him outgunned. Despite the fact that all of the business control and manpower actually fell under Scarfo as the family head, I had direct control of the businesses from early on, as well as the allegiance of the men that come under my control. Scarfo's unknown strengths were his men in the Philly area and whatever connections he had with the other Bosses in the New York and northern Jersey families. Fortunately wars between family members were costly in lost manpower and money, and the Commission discouraged all out conflict against another family unless permission is given, and it is rarely given. It is much more common that individuals are removed by force, and it is less costly and disruptive for business income.

CASINOS IN ATLANTIC CITY

After the Bill passed to allow casinos to be built in Atlantic City, Resorts International planned to build a Hotel Casino complex and would be Atlantic City's first casino to open in America outside of Las Vegas. This newest source of revenue stream would take a different set of approaches from me in order to partake in a percentage of the casino's revenue. I would need my contacts in the city government to apply pressure on Resorts Hotel and Casino. This special type of leverage took time to develop, but permitted me to receive a small piece of the action. Our slice of profits from their operation would continue to increase over the following months and years from milking the casino profits. This would keep Scarfo satisfied while those details were negotiated and the money was running upstream from the new source.

In 1975 New Jersey passed the Bill to allow gambling in casinos on the ocean boardwalk and adjoining properties. With promises of the level of grandeur that Las Vegas enjoys, and a possible similar revenue stream it could bring to the state. These were a few of the reasons the Bill passed. Having gambling in Atlantic City meant the population from New York and Philadelphia wouldn't have to catch a flight to Las Vegas.

Since most visitors would be day trippers, there was a steady gambling money stream, without having to rely on the hotel rooms being rented. Thousands of people could drive to Atlantic City then drive home after gambling for the day.

I wasn't that interested in actual ownership of the casino business because to succeed you needed to go real big, and that took big bucks and lots of influential people in your pocket. I make a lot of money, but there is money, and there's big money, and I didn't fall into the big money bracket. What I did have was the other side of the equation; influential people in my pocket. So being in this new position with the Mob I didn't have to own a casino or hotel in order to reap the big money.

The Resorts International had their ribbon cutting in 1978 with Steve Lawrence and Eydie Gorme, his wife, being the headliners in the theater. Steve Lawrence was the first person to roll the dice at the craps table, and lost $50.00 on the first two rolls. The casino was off to a good start! In addition to the casino there was a nine-hundred room hotel that was completely booked the first day, and every other hotel, rooming house, and apartment in the entire Atlantic City area was rented. The casino had seventy-five thousand people pass through their doors that day, most just wanting to take a look, but the gamblers kept the tables and slot machines at full capacity. It didn't take long for the table limits to reach twenty-five dollars for each play. That's expensive, creating a very profitable Grand Opening. Jack Cowen was the president and James Simon was the chairman of Resorts International, and for me to break into some of the generated funds this hotel casino was to make, it would be necessary for me to get close to one of them and identify their weakness, wants or needs. I needed that information to apply pressure on them so they would willingly give me a steady stream of insurance money. Selling the insurance shouldn't be a problem since the city's mayor, some of the council, and a good portion of the police force were already on my payroll. Using code citations, parking violations and frequent inspections by the Health Department, would give me leverage on the casino. If that isn't enough, our labor union connections which provided the workforce could cripple the hotel casino.

I thought the Resorts International president Jack Cowen, was the man to negotiate with because he was in charge of the casino floor and hotel on a daily basis. Jack had the most day-to-day knowledge of anyone at Resorts, and therefore, he was making the daily decisions.

After many face-to-face meetings, Jack and I came to an understanding on the terms of our business together. I was able to get the percentage of the casino revenue I demanded, and a different agreeable percentage of the hotels income, in exchange for special attention and protection for the Resorts International. Other hotel casinos had already applied for gambling licenses and building permits for hotels. Jack knew I could delay those applications on all fronts. I was also able to provide a full labor force that he needed to run his operation. This was a good day!

KELLY'S BAR

I was constantly moving my business location for security reasons, not from the police but from stupid thugs that might think they could make big money from robbing my counting rooms. I refer to this type of individual as stupid, since it would be very unwise to try to get through the heavily armed guards each counting room had, and the reinforced doors, walls and windows, with electronic surveillance equipment each room contained. Besides that, the extensive network surrounding my organization identified and tracked many of the trouble makers entering Atlantic City, and reported back to me if a possible problem was anticipated.

In spite of what I thought was high security, I still moved the counting rooms from time to time. My newest spot was my recent purchase on Columbia Place which was one block from the boardwalk where the Steel Pier was located. I bought a small narrow building that housed Kelly's Bar. I bought the bar mainly because of my mom Sarah. She moved out of Philly and came to live with me in the empty spare bedroom shortly after Papa died earlier that year. I thought this would be a major infringement on my life, but it turned out to be a non-event, because after Papa died she couldn't deal with daily life. All she wanted to do was go to work with me every day! Each morning I would help her get up on her bar stool, which was the furthest away from the front door and overlooked the pool table. Sarah was a short, thin, eighty-one year old woman. Mom had very black dyed hair and wore heavy makeup. She always wore her heels and a black party dress that was in vogue thirty years prior, and it had seen better days. Her position at the bar was always in the same spot at the end of the bar. With one arm on the bar she would smoke her cigarettes, and have a short glass of rail vodka she would sip on throughout the day. She sat with her legs crossed while she looked around the bar unless a pool game was in progress. Her attention then would be on the table for every shot. It didn't seem as if she minded the long days at the bar on that stool as long as she could be close to her Tony. Occasionally someone would ask her how things were going and that would prompt a big smile and a head nod to acknowledge the question. Short as the encounter may have been, it still brightened up her mood.

Entering through the front door of Kelly's, the bar was located on the left side running three quarters the length of the building. On the right just inside near the front there were four high top tables with two stools at each table. Halfway back on the right side was one pool table with a couple of high bar stools and an old single leather chair shoe shine stand. At the very back on the right was an ancient phone booth with a bi-fold etched glass entry door, and a small metal corner shelf located under the pay telephone. A metal seat was provided as well as an overhead light and fan that came on automatically when the bi-fold glass door was pulled closed.

When entering the bar from the bright sunlight during the day, it would take awhile for the eyes to adjust to the darkness of the space. The ambiance of the building was enhanced by the dark bar and dark walls which was fully stocked with four tiers of various liquors. The front of the bar had fifteen stools without backs. The high top tables were for dining or when the customers just wanted to get a little privacy from the bartender and other patrons, since this bar was a locals drinking hole and everyone knew each other. Dining was available, but the term dining was misleading since the only real food was a meatball or sausage hoagie with gravy. Of course, there were the requisite large jars of either pickled pigs feet, pickled pigs knuckles, or pickled hard boiled eggs, colored red by beet juice.

In the far rear of the long narrow building on the left was a one-stall bathroom which accommodated both sexes and was always in need of cleaning. On the bar side, across from the pool table was a door without a sign that if opened, you would be facing an entire wall of hooks with over a hundred keys hanging on them. These keys went to buildings that I owned or managed. They were tagged for identification, but I knew which keys were for each property since I acquired them one by one over the years. It was one of my daily routines to give keys to one of my men that needed to visit various properties for good or not-so-good reasons. Beyond the wall of keys was a small room not any larger than a walk-in closet that held a roll top desk and a well-worn leather recliner with a blanket covering the back, arms and seat of the chair. Everyone knew this was my chair, so no one else sat there. This bar office was where I spent the majority of the day while my accountant sat at the desk counting and recording thousands of dollars each day. Every flat space in that room had stacks of collected cash from around Tony Capra's empire.

The money was delivered throughout the day from the

various business ventures with some of the deliveries coming right through the front door and through the bar. But most came through the back door leading to the alley. You would think that with a desk, a recliner and two people in a small space, it would be crowded, and it was. But add in one more person, Angie, whose duty was to receive the bags of money from the runners, and that made working conditions real close. Wherever there weren't stacks of bills, there were piles of ledgers presumably for those receivables paid for by checks or credit cards. We must keep it legal for the IRS!

Kelly's bar served mostly draft beer and shots of whiskey. There was a wide assortment of other hard liquors and bottled beers, although most of the locals stayed with the program of shots and beer. A customer could also place a bet on different horse racing tracks around the country, and of course play the daily number. Neither the bartender nor any other employees of the bar sold those products. I kept a guy posing as a customer at the bar or a table making the transactions. This method kept the bar and myself out of trouble with regards to my liquor license in case we got raided. And also kept us out of jail.

MY GIRLS

Another money making business of mine was prostitution. Before the Resorts International opened, I had three or four full time prostitutes that I would put up in one of the rooming houses and charge them rent. They used the rooms to turn their tricks and kick back a sizable portion of each transaction: a pretty lucrative deal. After Resorts opened, if more girls were needed to cover large events such as conventions, I would contact as many as twenty part-time hookers to handle the extra business. You may be surprised to hear the term part-time hooker, but we had a pool we could contact. They were more than happy to take a break from their full time jobs as secretaries, housewives and stay at home moms to make a few extra bucks lying on their backs entertaining the visitors.

Resorts International changed my call-girl business. Instead of three or four full time prostitutes I had thirty full-time girls and the part-time list expanded three times the number we used to run. In addition there was also a demand to have male hookers available. The bonus of having all of the extra girls working at the increased hourly fees that had tripled, created the enormous revenue that portion of my business generated.

There was another advantage of handling top rated, high earning beautiful prostitutes besides the vast income they produced. They also provided a source of female company and sexual release that I needed at times. I never married, or even had a steady girl after High School. I really, never had the time. My time was consumed running my business and making money. When the need arose, and I had the time, I just went to my stable of girls and had a pretend date and any kind of sex I wanted. I paid with a big tip and went back to work. It was mechanical for both of us, and after we were finished, there were no necessary social requirements such as "I'll call you," or "Could I give you a ride home?" None of that. Once the money changed hands the transaction was complete and neither party had to say a word. There was no "Thank You" or "Goodbye." It was done.

CASINO OWNER

Prior to the Resorts International being built I didn't have any desire to be an owner of a casino hotel. Not that I didn't want the additional income, it was just a bigger nut than I could put together at the time to develop such a venture that size. But now that I had a large stash of cash and I had the income from the boardwalk rooming houses and single story flats that I had been accumulating over the past years, it might be possible.

With the blessing of the Mayor, several council members, and the head of the zoning board, it was only a few weeks before I had my properties vacated, the buildings leveled and fence barriers installed. The plans for the hotel casino had been filed and permits were approved and issued, never in Atlantic City has the building process been so fast. Ground breaking ceremonies took place three weeks later on the hotel casino that was to be named The Piedmont Hotel.

Attending the ceremony with shovels in hand was the mayor, some council members, other prominent business owners and Johnny Rinzo, all digging a shovel full of dirt and throwing it aside. The construction had started. I had Johnny represent me at the ceremony because I was still very serious about living a low keyed existence and watching my back from those that wanted to displace me and take over my organization. Hell, I still lived above the Pizza shop in a two bedroom apartment with my mother! I believe if you pay attention to the small details, the large details will take care of themselves.

I have to admit that when the construction got rolling, my cash was depleting at an alarming rate, though not any faster than I had anticipated. But I still didn't like my money leaving, even if it was for my own project. One of the unsavory decisions I was pushed into was to use the concrete pouring company that Scarfo owned: The same construction company he owned and used to ascend to the head of the Family. I used my own money and real estate to develop this project, now I'll have to use Scarfo's company, pay Scarfo's elevated charges for the concrete and brick work, and after the building and casino was up and running, Scarfo will expect a cut of the proceeds. I will wait for the right opportunity to displace him, but first I'll go along with his construction company doing the work and bide my time. This is my town and as tough as Scarfo might be, he will realize I will always come out on top.

My network of politicians, police, judges, city officials, and newspaper journalists is truly the strength of my organization. And that being said, I started delivering small bits of anonymous incriminating evidence connecting Scarfo to racketeering crimes to a few of my newspaper connections. There were many other major crimes Scarfo could be arrested for, but racketeering would nail him if the newspapers were tenacious, and he would land in jail.

As the hotel neared completion with the exterior of the building completed and the interior moving forward at a fast pace my money drain continued, but not as drastic as it was earlier. I was able to call in some favors and saved a lot of money for drywall and lumber. And when the furnishings were ready for the rooms, I got a break on that also. Seems the owner of a large furniture chain didn't want me to tell his wife and friends the damaging information I had about his indiscretions he had with a twelve year old boy. I got one great deal on furniture.

Three weeks before the hotel casino construction was scheduled to be completed, Scarfo was arrested for various criminal charges, one of which was racketeering.

The legal system had a difficult job ahead, since the boss of a Mafia family had never been convicted of a major crime and had to serve time. One of the reasons is because of all of the dirty politicians, judges and such that the family has in their pocket. They are able to get to anyone, including the people serving on the jury. Even if Scarfo beats the charges and doesn't serve any time, he will be out of my hair for quite awhile until he gets free from the depositions, investigations, attorney consultations and newspaper scrutiny.

EXPANDING TERRITORY

My operation was running smoothly on all cylinders. The only concern was how to launder the vast amount of cash that was flowing in. Soon after Scarfo got tied up trying to untangle his legal mess, I contacted the other heads of the Atlantic City and Philly operations. Two of them were smaller than mine, and one that extended into Philly was larger. My intention was to take their operations and roll them into mine, by simply announcing that they would now be answering to me instead of Scarfo. If that didn't work I was going to take them by force.

The advantage I had over the other family heads was the number of armed men on the street and the number of politicians and judges I had in my control. When I notified them they would be reporting to me in the absence of Scarfo, I didn't expect all three to just roll over and accept this from me without a fight, and I was correct. Frank Esposito headed the Philly operation and a piece of the southern tip of Jersey. He decided not to send an answer back to me while the other two did and agreed to my terms. Instead I heard on the streets that Frank was hiring more men, and purchasing more guns. He was beefing up protection on his gambling and money counting locations. He was on the defensive, and it was now my turn to make a move.

I called Johnny Rinzo to my office and directed him to assemble our best ten men, and visit Frank Esposito at his bar in Philly where he is known to do business. I told him to eliminate him and anyone that gets in the way and to be completely positive Frank was in the bar: If not, abort the mission.

Seven hours later that night Johnny knocked on my door, came in and sat down in the chair across from me. I poured him a shot of Four Roses whiskey and slid it across the desk to him, asking how it went. Johnny said the job was successful, but we lost one of our men. I said that I was sorry, but sometimes it was unavoidable. We clinked our glasses as a toast and drank to success. In the following days my operation absorbed the three territories, and I put someone I trusted in charge of Esposito's former territory.

I was doing my best to keep a low profile with regards to my powerful sprawling organization. I was now the Boss of the Southern Jersey and Northern Philly territories that came to fruition as a result of strong arm tactics and purging key heads of Scarfo's organization.

I was in control of the casino business on the East Coast, and Atlantic City was the tourist destination for Philadelphia and New York, bringing thousands to the shore. It is certain the Five Families of the New York and Chicago Commission will be eyeing my business as a possible growth acquisition. Now more than ever it's imperative that I watch my back. Ever since we put the hit on Frank Esposito, we had a steady flow of his followers coming at us seeking revenge or trying to retake Frank's business for themselves. I am fortunate to have a good crew who were able to fend off any possible attempts of a takeover.

One of the effective ways the Mafia family put pressure on other family heads was to abduct close friends or family members and threaten them with harm or death. Often it wasn't a threat. Knowing this, I always feared about someone getting to me through my mom Sarah, and threaten to cause her harm. This was definitely my weakest link, and therefore a possible way to take over my Atlantic City kingdom. To ease my mind, I added three more heavily armed men to protect her at Kelly's Bar, with orders to blend in and not be obvious bodyguards.

Business was good and there weren't any overthrow attempts on my territories. In fact we routinely entertained other Mafiosi visitors from the other top families from New York, Philadelphia, and Chicago. Important men such as Frank Costello, and members from Lucky Luciano's crime family and the Gambino Family. My network alerted me as soon as they hit town. I would go and greet them, invite them to my casino, comping them with free play, as well as other casinos I had leverage over. I also comped restaurant meals, and call girls.

I never picked up on anything that would indicate trouble for me. There was no hint of jealousy or any sly remarks about my success, so I felt relieved I wasn't being being targeted. But I will still be vigilant about watching my back and keeping my relationships secret.

My mom Sarah died of a heart attack a few months after I increased the security for her. She died at Kelly's Bar, sitting on the same stool she always sat on, with a cigarette in her hand and a short glass of vodka next to her elbow.

There wasn't a viewing for her, just the cemetery graveside service. I didn't advertise who she was and made no mention of our relationship. I had to keep it secret. If I had advertised my mother had died and gave details there would have been a hundred people show up, for the sole reason of paying me respect, not to say goodbye to her. I did not want that for her, and I didn't need to chance the exposure. At the cemetery grave site were a handful of the bar customers that had grown to know her over the years as a fixture of the bar. I will miss her dreadfully, but now I have no one to worry about being tortured or killed in order to get to me. I can now be more aggressive with business, I have nothing else to think about, and no reason to even go home anymore. I will be a constantly moving target. Only Johnny will know where I was at any given time, and everyone had to go through him first. I felt safe.

WHITE POWDER

The sales of cocaine was the money king on the street. Larger amounts of marijuana was being sold, but the product was more bulky and the cost per transaction was so much less than cocaine. The sale of cocaine, or "coke", was sold to a number of steady buyers, and there was also a small percentage of buyers wanting to try it for the first time. The sale of Marijuana was very dependable, and sold to customers that provided a very steady sales base. Some of the larger buyers were buying from us to sell to their customers after cutting the product by adding things such as dried grass, parsley, or anything else they could find to stretch the ounce of marijuana. I didn't care what the customer did with product once we had their money, unless their business interfered with my business.

Another sector we dealt in were pills. We probably had more and better access to a variety of pills than most pharmacies, and of course charged more than the pharmacies, because insurance companies did not pick up the tab – our customers did.

Heroin was starting to make a foot hold on the street. This was due to existing drug users needing to advance to a stronger level of high that marijuana or coke could not provide.

Over half of my prostitutes were hooked on the stuff. I got the money from the sale of heroin to them, but when they were on out of control highs and lows, it sometimes disrupted their ability to perform, and that affected my business. I replaced many of the girls hooked on the drug in order to get control over that situation. It was quite a disruption in the call girl sector until the turnover of working girls was completed. It was necessary for my ladies to be absolutely clean of hard drugs. In the long run it proved to be great for the business since word got out among customers that my girls were clean from disease and drugs, which made for a safer, and costlier transaction.

OPPOSITE DIRECTION

In February of 1973 word was that Frank Costello had died. No details were known, but when a giant of the Mafia dies, you can't help to pause and realize it could have easily been you instead. Not many at that level die from old age.

One thing for certain was that when one of the heads of the Families got whacked, there was a replacement waiting to take his place. Usually it was the same person that arranged for the Family head to have been killed in the first place.

I was the boss of my family for Atlantic City and northern Philadelphia and had total control of all the illegal businesses in those territories. At times families in the New York and Chicago territories have tried strong arm tactics to expand into my operational area. I quickly discouraged their attempt to accomplish that by force simply by opposing their threat with a greater amount of force. During those attempts, business always suffered for a time because it took my men away from their duties of collecting cash. Squashing these disruptions quickly were necessary in order to dissuade outsiders from trying to cut into our business. Sure, lives were lost on both sides protecting the operation, but that could not be helped. Examples had to be made to the other families trying to push their way into my city, and the message had to be known on the street that it wasn't easy to attempt a takeover of my family. I would not roll over easily.

Business couldn't be better, with an abundance of cash I continued accumulating properties, my family continued to grow and was now expanding into many legal ventures. The key advantage I had in expanding my empire so fast was due to my long list of prominent people in powerful positions that I had leveraged, and for that reason the cash kept piling up. So where do I go from here to seek more power. I had no desire to rise to the head of the New York or Chicago families. I was very content with my compact productive kingdom. I didn't have the desire to be a target of a hit, nor have any additional exposure from authorities wanting to take me and my business down. I didn't want to constantly watch out for the ambitious young and upcoming hoodlum that wants to take over my territory and be the new boss. So I decided to go in the opposite direction. I would pursue politics, and the Senate should be the office that provides me the best opportunities. Networking with powerful individuals in government would allow me to identify their flaws and use that information to gain leverage over them and their offices. Therefore advancing my empire and at the same time casting a legitimate veil over it.

The hardest task of becoming a politician for me was the exposure of running for office. Being a politician after winning an election wouldn't be that difficult as I already possessed most of the attributes needed. I am cunning, influential, crooked, and can convince others to do anything I want them to do. All I need is someone that knows how to run a winning campaign. That search with the assistance from a couple of my contacts in The House of Representatives, led me to an attorney, Gordon Stein, who operated two offices in New Jersey. My contacts said he was very well connected in the political scene, and worked on the last three major campaigns. One campaign was for state Governor, and two were for members of the House. All three won their elections. I was also told he would go to any measures to win a contest. Sounds like I found myself a Campaign Manager.

Gordon Stein didn't waste any time getting to work setting up my campaign machine. We were late getting into the race, and only had fifteen months until Election Day. Gordon took care of everything, such as hiring our staff and assigning the volunteers to duties, making all arrangements for in-person Town Hall gatherings, ground-breaking ceremonies, baby kissing, and other stuff that had to be done to get the people and Press to notice me. Gordon knew all the angles of this game, and he knew who he had to pressure in order to get what he wanted. He would have made a good mob boss. He was very effective.

At first I went about my every day duties with my private sector organization, and didn't have to think about running for office. Gordon or his right hand girl would call to tell me I had to be at a new store or a restaurant grand opening event, or perhaps make a speech at some gathering of the Knights of Columbus. The minor scheduling commitments for me didn't interfere with my main business at all. In fact my business was running very well without any problems, and that made me a little nervous. In my line of work there are always adjustments that need to be made to personnel that have stepped out of line; sometimes minor adjustments, sometimes major permanent adjustments. But this quiet period is unsettling. Is somebody planning to upset my cart before I get into office, or is there someone in the wing that has their eye on replacing me and taking over my business.

I will reach out to my network for answers; if either is being planned, I will find out.

Fortunately none of the inquiries I sent out to my organization came back positive, which means nobody is planning to upset my plans to run for office nor planning an attempt to infringe on my business. That information put me somewhat at ease, but now that I suspected something might be working in the background, I will be extra vigilant watching for any deviations in my money making machine.

The following months leading up to election day proved to be more challenging than I expected. Gordon's assistant Gloria, kept me busy with in-person visits to a multitude of fraternal and non-profit organizations. I gave speeches at the American Legions and Food for Pets, and everything in between. There were many groups I never even heard of, but I catered to each of them and designed my speech to whatever they wanted to hear me say. That's politics: find out what a group with like thinking wants to change, and tell them that it is your priority to accomplish once in office. It doesn't matter what change they seek. The wish list went from parking space matters to cleanup of a vacant lot, to lower property taxes or higher unemployment checks.

My platform is a moving one, since I change my priority issues depending on which group of voters I was addressing. The consistent platform promise every group wanted was to lower taxes for the middle and lower income groups, and to clean up crime and corruption in our state. The effort visiting groups of voters wasn't a hardship, in fact I was able to discover new areas to get involved in to bring additional investments for my business. What did put me in a bind was the time element. Before I decided to run for office I was already working an average of seventeen hours per day managing my business, so any time taken away from my main show presents an element of weakness. Fortunately, I was aware of being vulnerable during this year of campaigning and made adjustments. I already have the tightest of loyal crews in my organization, so all I had to do was to rearrange the pecking order a little, and that provided overlapping reporting responsibilities, which increased the checks and balance. So far the tweaking of the reporting was working great with no objections from any of the crew. This is working so well that after I am elected, I will probably keep the new structure.

The exposure I got from Town Hall meetings and the many fraternal organization visits provided me with many new supporters, and created a growing base of support for my election hopes. My influence with a few of the largest newspapers in Jersey, and Gordon's knowledge of how to exactly spin the stories we wanted the public to know, provided leverage over the other candidates. This tactic worked for me, but couldn't work as easily for my opponents because my public life has been muted for many years, and very few individuals know anything about me or my business. I have no known history since I kept so many layers of separation between how I make my money, what I do with it, and my crew that makes it happen for me. It would take an enormous amount of diligence to uncover any dirt on me. I never married and all of my relatives are dead, so with no wife or kids, there isn't any chance for information that may harm me accidentally leak out to the public.

Having control of the newspapers permitted the blockage of any derogatory news about me being printed. When we needed to spread or make up targeted news about my opponents, that news would be the featured story. If by some chance a small rogue newspaper decided to print something derogatory about me or someone in my campaign, my crew took care of it using various effective convincing methods.

With seven weeks to go before election day, the field of candidates running for the Senate has narrowed down to two individuals. One is me and the other is Clayton Kerry. Clayton is a second generation Irish guy from Camden, New Jersey. He is married with six children, and has been in politics most of his adult life, working his way up the ladder which began as a representative of his home township. He steadily moved forward to his last served office term in the House of Representatives. He is much more qualified for the Senate position than I am, and his reason for running is much different than mine. Clayton wants to promote the State of New Jersey, while I want to promote the machine of Tony Capra. The shame of the matter is that Clayton would make an excellent Senator, but the election is only for one Senator, so he must lose this time around.

Clayton's support is from his political party's muscle. Strong, but no match for my available money and real muscle.

MAFIA FEARS

A s election day draws closer, I have been informed that some of the bosses from the New York and Chicago Families are concerned about the possibility of my winning the Senate race. The polls have me twenty-five percent ahead of Clayton Terry, and with the increased voter support it can become a reality. Their concern was due to not knowing how much damage I could cause to their interests by having that much control and leverage in the office of Senator. They were worried I could undermine their strength in business, and therefore weaken their stronghold and lower the organization's income.

TURN OF EVENTS

With only three weeks to go before election day, I was scheduled to give a speech at the Rotary Club brunch which was located just outside of Atlantic City. The large hall was packed with all of the tables filled, and standing three deep with reporters and potential voters around the back and sides of the room.

My reception at the Rotary Club was welcoming with four minutes of standing applause. A good supportive start to the visit. I was about halfway through my written speech when a guy came from my left and walked quickly until he reached the front of the podium where he raised the pistol he had in his hand and shot me in the chest twice. The man continued in the same direction running. The surprise of the event prevented any of my protection detail from getting a shot at him in the crowded room. He was able to disappear out a side door that opened into the ally and got away.

When I was shot I collapsed immediately and blanked out, and fortunately there were two Rotary member attendees at the brunch who were doctors that came to my aid until an ambulance team arrived and started an I V and applied proper bandages. The ride to the hospital was short, and I was taken directly into the operating room.

I remained unconscious for four days and was now recovering in the hospital with a large contingent of my crew on-site protecting me and guarding the area. My patient chart indicated I was in stable condition, and had emerged from the coma. I later found out the bullets just grazed the tip of my lung and missed any other vital organs. Doctors said I was extremely lucky, but I had already come to that conclusion because it is rare anyone ever survives a hit from the mob.

Recuperating in the hospital after being ambushed and shot gave me plenty of time to think and reflect on how my situation has changed trying to balance between running for the Senate and being a crime boss. Up until now I have always lived my adult life in secrecy and maintaining an extremely low profile which enabled me to be invisible to the public eye. The main reason this was possible was because I ran all of my operations through my trusted hand-picked associates.

Prior to getting shot I only needed to protect my connection to organized crime from the other political party. Finding any dirt on my private or government life would provide opposing individuals the ability to have leverage over me and cause my demise in public office, as well as the destruction of my private empire. But for now the attention of the media was focused on the man running for Senator being shot by an assassin while at a public political rally at the Rotary Club. This front page story provided a reason for many reporters across the country to dig into my private life to find every detail there was about this unknown candidate. The media would be tenacious in trying to find any damning background information on me, especially if there are not any obvious details to write their exposé. I considered taking the chance that the media wouldn't uncover damaging information, or I could feed them the story they wanted to hear and print.

I opted for the later and chose to give an exclusive interview to one of the newspaper contacts I have in my pocket. After meeting with him, we were able to fabricate an article that created an all American boy from humble roots with a dream to serve his country and protect its citizens from the wrath of organized crime. My reporter concluded his article stating that I was shot because of the pressure of my campaign promises to rid New Jersey of organized crime was getting too intense for the Mobsters. The reality is the crime families were getting too much attention and were worrying about me getting elected and gaining excessive power in the government, and then using that power to take them down, and allowing me to replace their criminal organizations with my own.

It wouldn't take long to find out if the fabricated article we floated out to the media would be enough to satisfy the thirst to find the underlying facts they sought. I figured a week was the amount of time I had to wait to see if the story took hold. America's public attention doesn't last more than a couple of days before another story takes the limelight and everyone moves on to a new subject of interest as it turns out, it only took a few days before my story was pushed aside by another story about a severe winter storm in the Dakotas.

I spent three weeks in the hospital before being released. I was sore and very weak from the operation and lying on my back for too long, but I will work on that when I get home. I wasn't going to go to my primary home above the pizza parlor because I thought the steps might be difficult for me to navigate at this time. The other reason was that I needed a place where my crew could be close enough to me in order to protect me from a possible mob retry on my life.

SAFE HOUSE

Prior to announcing my run for the Senate, I purchased a large split-level house in the suburbs outside of Atlantic City. The property was on a rural road sitting on two acres with a long driveway leading up to the house. There was a pond on the left side that bordered the property line from the street all the way back to where the lot ended. Along the rear property line was an eight foot stone wall that had been constructed during the Civil War for a plantation house that had burned down. On the right side were closely planted double line rows of pine trees that ran from the street all of the way back to the stone wall. In between the rows of pines, I had barbed wire fences installed for added security. The perimeter was fairly secure to restrict any unwanted entry easily.

I purchased this house and property in order to have an address that was not connected with my business, and was one hundred percent legitimate for all of the inquiring eyes seeking information about me during the election. Since an attempt had been made on my life, I will be using the residence as a safe house. It's unfortunate that the attempt on my life wasn't at my safe house instead of the Rotary Club, as we would have the dead bodies of the assassins to identify and connect to the mob boss that put out the ordered hit.

My organization was structured so that all of my individual businesses were able to function automatically without any direct supervision from me. The captains in each of my businesses report directly to Johnny Rinzo, who then reports to me. This was how we operated at the beginning, and now that the organization had grown exponentially, we still use the same proven method. This way I keep my hands on the pulse of my kingdom, while not being directly connected to any of the businesses. This type of leadership keeps me out of jail. This mode of operation works so well that most of the people on my payroll don't even know my name, let alone know what I look like, and that is the way I planned it.

With business continuing as normal, the campaign took an upward turn. Because of all the publicity I was receiving from being shot at the Rotary Club political rally, and running on the platform to remove organized crime from our state, my approval rating soared and elevated my chance of winning the election to Senate. I was the main news item, and many potential voters that never even paid attention to the race were now interested, and joined in support of my effort to win.

SENATOR CAPRA

I was still recovering in my Jersey safe house on election day when they announced the outcome. I had beaten my opponent. Every day I could feel my strength returning, and was told by my doctors I would not have any further damage as a result of the gunshot wounds. No vital areas had been hit and the healing was progressing well. One of the good things that came out of this ordeal was that I didn't have to campaign at all after being shot, yet my ratings soared to the top. It can't get any better than that.

As stated prior, I have been successful in keeping my criminal activities hidden from view, otherwise I never would have been elected to the US Senate. I was becoming a well liked, influential Senator, and enjoyed reaping the benefits of that office. The biggest advantage of being an elected Congressman was the ability to use the leverage of my office and position to apply pressure on various individuals, without the use of physical force. As a result, my illegal as well as legal business entities were able to thrive.

Campaigning for the Senate office I ran on various platforms in order to win votes. I made promises to the voters to address whatever issue they thought was important to them. The two common issues every group usually wanted addressed, was organized crime, and cleaning up our streets from drug use. At each meeting or rally I would strongly declare how important that was on my agenda, and promised to rid our cities and state of those maladies.

I know how outrageous that sounds since I was the Mafia Kingpin for the New Jersey and Philly region. But nobody in the public knew that, and that was what the voters wanted to hear.

I have been known to be able to identify an opportunity when others might not, and move on it quickly to gain the advantage. As I became more powerful as a Senator, the thought crossed my mind that I could possibly combine my promise to the voters to fight organized crime, and at the same time remove some of the key Mafia family heads that have wanted to move in on my territory and overthrow my empire. I always suspected the Chicago mob bosses of wanting to make a move on me, and although there isn't any proof, my gut tells me one of the Chicago bosses was behind the professional attempt on my life that day at the Rotary Club.

I decided to go through with a vendetta against the Chicago mob. It will be a very precarious road to navigate. I will have to be extremely careful being the instigator of an investigation into the Chicago Mafia's businesses, and the Mob's leaders. As a Senator, I used persuasion to get a committee formed to investigate organized crime. I then supplied insider information about the mob to the committee, which saved several months or even years to obtain the same information by normal means. My name was kept out of the news as a key Senator making the probe because I gave the credit to other Senators.

A MOVE ON THE MOB

There are two obvious reasons why I don't want any credit for the actions taken against the mob. First of all the families in Chicago and New York know me, and have been watching my moves closely ever since I got elected. All of the families have been worried about possible threats to their business from me being in such a powerful position in government. Hence the attempted hit on my life. They are very aware of Senator Tony Capra being as much a criminal as they are, with as much to lose if things go badly. That knowledge gives them a small sense of ease knowing that if they go to prison, I will most likely be right next to them in the adjoining cell.

I must not be seen connected with the probe because every mob family has connections with the newspapers in their territories, and Chicago is no exception. With their news media contacts in Chicago and New York, they could fabricate a smear campaign on me and cause my whole house to fall.

Another reason for staying in the background of the investigation is that if the probe spreads outside of the targeted Chicago mob heads, it could possibly backfire by spreading to my business ventures, and that also would bring my house down.

I realized how difficult it would be to accomplish this move on the Mob. Coming up with a flawless plan to bring down the Chicago Mob required working out the many intricate details that must transpire for the planned probe to be successful. Thinking about the many different scenario's that could occur and adversely affect me, helped me make my decision. It's the challenge itself that convinced me to go through with the scheme.

During the following days the plan was constantly fine tuned to ensure the probe would be successful, and at the same time not have any downside to my interests. My next step was to propose the plan to the proper Senators to form a committee. There isn't any anticipated problem a committee will be formed, since I have a couple of the key members in my pocket. Feeding them the insider information on the Chicago bosses provided the process a huge jump start.

The committee members are career politicians, and any legislation they propose against the Mafia is a huge boost for their political future.

Even with the insider evidence provided about the Chicago bosses, the process took months due to the numerous investigations and the legislation moving from committee to committee. Finally the committee had enough information to issue the Chicago bosses subpoenas to appear before the Grand Jury.

This was not the first time the Mafia went before the Grand Jury, and when it happened previous convictions had been avoided. This time however, this Grand Jury found verified criminal offenses to convict the one mob boss that appeared. The other boss that was served fled the country, and was presumed to be in Sicily. A warrant for his arrest was issued, but will most likely never be served.

During the following months the government was pressuring the Chicago Families, my business representatives worked in the background placing steady pressure on the Chicago territories. They raided their counting rooms, and forced takeovers of their largest income businesses. This was accomplished without much resistance because the Family heads were preoccupied covering their asses as a result of the Government probe into their criminal activity.

With the one boss fleeing the country to avoid prosecution, and the other boss being easily convicted, I was able to accumulate a sizable portion of their Chicago territories without sparking a gang war. The takeover of the territories was not seen by the families as a hostile move. The actions taken by my men were designed to seem as a way of assisting the boss that was under Government scrutiny. This was accomplished by taking over the sectors of their business that would prove the most devastating to him if he was found to be associated. He actually believed I was his savior, and was truly helping him. My scheme was working perfectly.

The end result of the probe and trial was successful due to my business maneuvers to take over the two Chicago territories as mob boss Tony Capra, coupled with my efforts to work in the background as Senator Tony Capra to get Salvatore Pino convicted. Pino was given twelve years to serve in a minimum security prison.

Following the conviction, I reorganized the two territories with my own leaders. Thirty per cent additional business was realized in the Chicago territory, and income was expected to increase by that percentage as well.

The Senate committee concluded their investigation with the conviction proceeding. The public reaction was positive, and regarded as a huge success. It was a win-win situation for all parties involved, except of course the mob boss, Salvatore Pino.

The best component of the entire probe plot was that no one knew I had initiated the probe that set up the eventual downfall of the Chicago bosses. Triumph was obtained by staying out of the limelight, which was necessary to protect my real business association, as well as my political identity as a Senator. Everyone in government office at that time profitted from that conviction of the Mafia head, by increasing their political clout with the voters.

Performing my duties as a Senator, such as signing onto various Bills produced benefits to citizens around the country, especially my state of New Jersey. Benefits such as infrastructure, crime prevention, and better schools. Even without trying, I was actually doing something good for the voters that elected me.

A SNITCH

The months following my strategic coup taking over some of the Chicago territories proceeded without major trauma, although some of my business entities were suffering from above normal government raids which was affecting my income. Using my influence as a Senator and using individuals in various government offices that owed me favors, I was able to probe for information without anyone knowing it was me asking. After a few days I found out there was a high level snitch in my organization that was supplying the FBI with my operations details. This type of problem arises occasionally and occurs every several months or so, but must be taken as a serious threat each time lest it has a chance to spread. Knowing from my government sources this was an insider, and which businesses were affected helped narrow the identity of the person or persons giving the FBI the confidential information. I summoned Johnny Rinzo and after sharing a couple of tall glasses of bourbon informed him of the breach and what I knew. Johnny said he was unaware of any extra government pressures but would check to see if we had any weak links in those businesses.

Weeks went by and Johnny found nothing to report, but the raids had significantly diminished. I was wondering if the FBI was informed by the person snitching that I was on to them, or did things just tighten up after Johnny was making inquires within those businesses. Either way, I still didn't have definitive answers to act on in order to fix the problem.

There was a lot on my plate these days. I was an active Senator, as well as the Mob boss for the New jersey and greater Philadelphia territories, and the newly acquired Chicago syndicate. Keeping everything running like a well-oiled machine was important for the survival of all parts. That's why the FBI pressure must be shut down, and I needed to find the cause of why it began in the first place.

I was working with Johnny Rinzo reorganizing those businesses compromised from the FBI raids. Together we were able to eliminate most of the obvious weaknesses and implement new security routines. Of course part of the fix came from performing a manpower shuffle, and certain eliminations. While Johnny was engaged in actively transforming the new business operation structure, he was informed that one of his Captains in that business had been seen with a known FBI agent at a rest area on the Jersey Turnpike. As instructed, Johnny brought the information to me before confronting the Captain. This time there wasn't any necessity for us to meet. We had discussed our plan of action during our first meeting. First Johnny would use all means to verify the accused was our informant. Second, if he was the informant, make certain that there wasn't an FBI protective plan for him in case his cover was blown. Third, if both the first and second steps were correct, then we would arrange for him to go missing permanently. A day later Johnny found a replacement Captain for that arm of that business, and all was good within the empire once again.

I was Seventy-Two the last week of May but I feel the same as I did when I was in my early sixties. I haven't developed any serious physical problems as of yet, which is a real mystery since the only exercise I get is walking around the casino floor and visiting my various owned properties in Atlantic City. My nutrition is questionable since I only eat in restaurants and from food carts, and I never take supplements or vitamins. On the other hand my consumption of alcohol is kept to a minimum, for clarity, not health. I don't have to worry about skin cancer resulting from sun exposure as I have never stayed outside very long. Unless research finds out that neon lights cause cancer, I'm safe.

NEW YORK GANG WAR

My empire is the largest and strongest it has ever been, with almost seventy percent of my business arms now legitimate. The only risk that could upset my success is the possibility of an all out gang war. This is a real possibility because the New York families are already engaged in war within their territories, and it has started to spread into the Chicago territory. The gang war spreading into Chicago will infringe on my ability to make the same profits I am making now, so I'll be forced to take sides, or be one of the sides against all of the other families at war. For the time being my Jersey and Philadelphia territories have been isolated from the New York upheaval. Gang wars usually start from the thirst and greed to have more assets than another family, or retaliation from a boss getting whacked. I plan to avoid getting involved if possible, because nobody wins in a war, and it is very costly.

Traveling back and forth between Washington, DC and Atlantic City, performing my duties as a Senator or Family Boss, and watching the expansion of the New York war, has all of my daily hours filled. I moved back to my flat above the pizza shop in Atlantic City where I felt the safest and my control was the strongest. My presence in my neighborhood is invisible to the public, even my several bodyguards manage to maintain a low profile and are able to blend in. I have never had a photo or video taken in over twenty years.

Preventing someone taking a photo or video since becoming a Senator has been hard. Even my official portrait has been postponed three times. I strive to remain invisible to everyone. It is necessary for my protection and existence.

I got the call from Johnny Rinzo after two o'clock in the morning telling me our largest numbers counting room in downtown Chicago, and a major counting room in Philadelphia had just gotten hit and everyone was killed in both locations. All money and slips were taken and the building was destroyed by fire: a total loss. I didn't respond immediately because I was calculating the numbers for this loss. When I did respond I asked Johnny if he had any idea who was to blame for the hit. Johnny said he already had feelers out for information and would know soon and get back to me as soon as he hears. With this aggression on my counting rooms, I'm in the war. This was the Mob's way to invite me into the fight. My hope that the war would stay confined to the New York area has now been crushed, and I find my family is at war. It has only been six years since the last multi-territory war, and those losses are gone forever.

HIT AGAIN

Later that evening Johnny called with the name of Paul Stalantos, a made man from the largest Chicago family, who also had strong ties in New York. Stalantos ordered the hit on my rooms and also had an accomplice with one of my captains in the Philadelphia territory. I told johnny to take care of our captain that betrayed us, and I would make a move on Stalantos. Before I was able to commence my plans to hit four of Stalantos key properties in Chicago and New York, word came through my network that one of my properties in Atlantic City would be be raided soon. Upon hearing this information, I summoned Johnny Rinzo to meet at my casino office. I took the short walk to the boardwalk casino from my Kelly's Bar office. I was about to enter through the security side door entrance that is closest to my casino office, when a shot rang out, followed by several other shots. I had been hit by two of the rounds, one in the leg and one in the shoulder. I collapsed to the ground. The other shots were at my bodyguards and the assailants. One of my guards lay dead next to me and all three of the gunmen were down and dead. With all of the shooting it wasn't long before Johnny and more of my men showed up. I was whisked into the casino and taken to my office where the casino nurse worked on stopping my bleeding and wrapping the wounds. I was whisked from the casino before the police showed up responding to the gunfight. My men took me to the small hospital I own just a few blocks off of the boardwalk. This hospital was a small, one doctor and one nurse brownstone house I had converted into a medical facility that was mainly used to serve the locals in the neighborhood at reduced prices. I kept this place to serve my needs for medical emergencies, and avoid going to the larger hospitals that are compelled to report stabbing and gunshot wounds to the police.

Dr. Mike stopped what he was doing as soon as we entered the building and came to my assistance with his nurse. I was taken into the treatment room where the nurse stripped off my pants and shirt and began cleaning the wounds while Dr. Mike set up the operating table trays with the tools he would need.

When I awoke after the operation the doctor told me I was very lucky because the two gunshots missed any vital organs, but recovery would take some time because of the muscle and bone damage to the areas hit. I acknowledged what he was telling me but it didn't register with me completely, probably due to the anesthesia effect I was coming out of.

The following morning I was much clearer in my thinking. I had coffee with Johnny who filled in the details that I didn't know. The first answers I wanted to know was if anyone other than my men saw me leave the casino, and how many people know where I am now. Johnny said only he and two other men saw me being carried away from the casino because everyone except for the men in the gunfight scattered as soon as the shooting began. As for the hospital, Dr. Mike and his nurse saw us when we brought you in. The only other person that was there was preparing to leave.

This was good news in regards to my safety. A very manageable level of exposure. Even if I had been seen, nobody knows who I am. In fact I won't be associated with the shooting episode for the same reason. The only person or persons that know I was at the scene are the ones that ordered the hit on me.

THE NEXT PLAN

Throughout my life I have prided myself on planning for every possible contingent that could go wrong in whatever venture I attempted. So while I was considering and planning what I would do in case I was shot again one day, or if I decided to disappear for various reasons, I came up with a plan which I will need to put into motion now.

My plan was to create a new identity and move to another country where I would live out my life as a retired accountant. Seven years ago I put my "in case of" plan together. The new identity was simple as I already had someone on my crew that took care of all of the fake documents I would need. The country of choice to move to initially was Sicily, Italy. After thinking it through I decided on Montreal, Canada because most of the mobsters that left America to escape for a variety of reasons wound up in Sicily. I couldn't take the chance of being exposed by another mobster on the run, and thrown right back into danger on my life.

In a quiet rural neighborhood on the outskirts of Montreal called Le Petite-Italie. I purchased a modest house on a big lot that had a separate bungalow a few yards from the main house. After I upgraded the house and bungalow with a new kitchen and bath and security features. I found an older Italian couple from the district of La Petite-Patr willing to move into the bungalow and maintain my properties. Dominic and Carmela were happy to be my employees, because they were paid in cash, had medical insurance, and lived there rent free.

The next part of my plan was for Johnny to disseminate the story that I was shot again and was killed. The newspapers wouldn't have any problem running the story about a Senator being assassinated, especially after the first failed attempt. The public as well as my fellow crime bosses will buy the story because there were no living witnesses to blow my cover. There will not be any services for anyone to attend because my wishes were to be cremated, and not have a wake, church service, funeral, cemetery, or memorial service.

Johnny secretly drove me to my house in Le Petite-Italie, Montreal where if everything goes as planned, I will be living out my retirement years with Dominic and Carmela tending to all of my needs.

After we arrived and we ate the fine meal Carmela prepared for us. Johnny and I went into the parlor and had a cigar and Bourbon. We discussed how Johnny Rinzo would become the new Don of my organization. With me being dead, there would surely be power struggles on a few fronts, especially the Chicago business. My advice to Johnny was to sever the interests in Chicago if the losses to manpower and profits became too high. Then concentrate on the Atlantic City region and fight hard to keep it intact because that is where the highest margins were. We both new the transition from the death of Tony Capra to Johnny Rinzo would be seamless since Johnny had been running the empire ever since I started the run for the Senate. My empire will survive and the cash flow will continue, but for me, not being able to have a direct control of my businesses will be the hardest part of this forced retirement.

During the following days after Johnny headed back to Jersey, I was touring around the adjoining Montreal districts, where I found the Port of Montreal District which reminded me of Atlantic City. It was on the water with a large percentage of Italians, and even it had a giant Gondola wheel, the La Grande Roue de Montreal. This Ferris Wheel cost almost Fifty dollars to take the ride. So money could be made here also. Everywhere I looked the businesses appeared legitimate, and I didn't see any indication of organized control. Sure there was crime, but there is some level of crime everywhere in the world. But all I was able to observe were a few minor hustles by a handful of thugs. With my new identity and my knowledge of how to organize, there might be an opportunity to create another empire here in Canada. I will keep it small by taking over the fragmented numbers games around the district, and acquire some men that aren't afraid to get their hands dirty and could handle a gun.

I will definitely give more thought to this idea, and put a plan together before I make any move to execute.

Other Books by Joe Myles

Fury: A Soldier's Journey (2019) is an autobiography in which Joe Myles covers the time he served in the US Army from 1967-1969 during the Vietnam War. Read about his combat stories—stories that have never been shared for fifty years.

Tony Capra: Organized Crime Boss (2024) is a fictional account of one man's rise through the mafia ranks. Follow Tony from his early childhood until becoming a man and discover how this innocent child is drawn into trouble by a seemingly lucrative opportunity that changes the direction of his life's path.

Patsy's Bedtime Stories (2024) is a whimsical fictional collection of short stories that were fabricated for pure entertainment and enjoyment.

www.ingramcontent.com/pod-product-compliance
Lightning Source LLC
Chambersburg PA
CBHW040017250626
47171CB00006B/37